Not A Real Love

Susan Blick

Ian's Pov :

Am I being stood up? Should I call her? Did she figure out my real intentions?

These questions kept on replaying in my mind as I waited for Maya. She is late, way too late. I have been waiting for her for half an hour. People in the restaurant kept looking at me with sympathy as if they thought that my "date" forgot about me. I felt so awkward. Is this Karma? Is the universe making me pay for all the girls that I stood up?

Should I ring her? or Just go to her house?

As I stood up, I heard my name being called and there she stood. Maya was dressed simply and she looked so delicate. My eyes roam her body studying and I noticed how she shifted her weight from one leg to another to show her discomfort. She is nothing like the girls I dated. She is nothing like the girl I love, Rose. Maya was simple. She didn't dress glamorously. She since the age of four hated attention and since her discomfort was clear, I knew for sure that she still hates it.

"Ian?" she repeated as I didn't respond to her but kept on eyeing all her small details. She is a girl and I am a player so my reaction to her appearance is totally normal no one needs to read much into it. As soon as my eyes reached her face, I saw smooth skin uncovered by makeup, plump lips coated in light pink gloss and then dark orbs that showed clear discomfort and that was enough to shake out of my trance.

"You are late." I blamed as I took my seat back

"I didn't want to come" she bluntly confessed which shocked me but also made me chuckle. She is as blunt as a kid.

"And why is that? Am I not charming enough for you Miss pure? Or is your boyfriend possessive of you?" I teased her as she took her own seat and my eyes yet again traveled to study her plump lips and curvy figure.

"Honestly, I don't get why you want to be friend me and Ian both of us know that you are not as charming as people think. You are just a typical player." she again spoke freely not caring about my reaction and my smirk was flipped upside down because right at moment I knew that getting her under my charm won't be that easy. This girl can certainly read me like an open book.

"I told you my reason. Rose, the person I trust the most said that you are the greatest friend there is." I tired to convince her of my not so real intentions even though Rose did really tell me about Maya and how great she is.

"I can recommend some other friends for you." Maya shot back while a small smile took over her lips.

"I want you." I insisted and her eyes rapidly met mine. Her intense gaze made me shiver. I wanted to break our gaze but somehow her eyes hypnotized mine and kept them in chained.

"Salut et Bienvenue chez "Chez Balzac". Je suis Bryan et je suis votre serveur. Voila les menus et je reviendrai en quelques minutes pour prendre vos commandes." A voice came from beside and shook me back to sanity.

I looked at the waiter to thank him but found that his eyes were sat on Maya. He didn't pay attention to me even when I thanked him but when Maya did he gave her in flirting smile. I felt uneasy watching such scene but decided to ignore it. Maya , on the other hand seemed clueless to the man who was eyeing her. Even when she thanked him, her eyes never left the tablecloth.

"He was flirting with you." I stated with a kind of a not so understandable hostility

"No he wasn't. Not all men are players, you know?" Maya replied shacking her head like a kid and that made me smile.

"But what if he was, will you give him a chance of a date?" I tried to convince her

"That's my business." She tried to sound rude but failed. It is simply not her nature.

"Come on May, are you afraid to answer a little question?" I teased her hoping for an answer.

"No I am not and just so you know I don't like the idea of dating strangers. If I truly knew his personality and found it intriguing then yes. I mean the guy looks good but that can't be enough." Maya explained as she eyed the waiter and I feared that he will get the wrong signals from her so I cleared my throat to get her attention.

"So what are you going to order?" I asked trying to start a normal conversation where we both stay civil.

"I would rather eat at Chipotle." Maya mumbled to herself but I heard her

"Not into fancy food?" I teased her but was also surprise because I am used to girls loving fancy restaurants.

"Not into fancy things in general. You know that the price of such meals can provide all week meals for a poor family?" Maya informed in a blaming way and her eyes once again connected with mine but were shooting me a look of blame.

"I do charity." I announced hating her blaming glare

"If you eat regularly here, then you are not doing enough for charity."She judged but why are her words affecting me so deeply?

"I will I promise." my words escaped my mouth and I nearly regretted them but when Maya smile sweetly at me I couldn't help but smile

"You are not so bad you know?" Maya continued to speak as she read the menu again but I saw her cheeks turn a bit pink, Is she blushing?

"Is that a compliment ?" I teased her more loving the effect I had on her and that's when the waiter decided to interrupt us.

"Vous avez choisi?" he questioned in a fake french accent and I found myself getting irritated with him

"Yes!" I replied rudely and continued to order what I wanted

"And you mademoiselle?" he turned back his attention to Maya as he finished taking my order and she replied nicely to him. Our lunch was served rapidly and we kept silent as we ate. Maya wasn't like the girls I dated, she didn't talk unless someone addressed her and I was a bit frustrated with her. How am I going to get close to her if she is not allowing me? How am I going to use her to get Rose jealous if she is not caring about me at all.

"What's wrong?" I asked as her eyes nearly popped in shock as she looked at her desert

"You were right!" she exclaimed holding a small paper and giving it to me.

I took the paper rapidly and found a neat written sentence in it "If your date goes wrong call me :(number). I don't know why but for a freaking unknown reason I wanted to punch that waiter. He thought that we were on a date but had the rudeness and audacity to openly flirt with Maya? I crumbled the paper and tossed in my water glass.

"That's unnecessary." Maya hushed

"He is rude and what did you want to call him?" I sounded angrier than needed but honestly I didn't care because maybe this kind of anger will be understood as possessiveness

" No but you could act more civilly. He was honest about his feelings so why disrespect him by showing him that his emotions are worthless...." she continued to argue but I didn't care and just shot a warning glare at the waiter.

"He asked not because of feelings but because of your look. He kept eyeing you since he laid his eyes on you." I tried to convince her but she just shook her head and refused to believe me.

Desert went as silent as lunch. We didn't talk and the only argument we had after that was about payment. Maya refused to let me pay for her and she stubbornly paid for herself and left a tip for Bryan. She even shot an apologetic smile to him as we went out.

"You are a real goody two shoes" I teased as we went out to the parking lot

"Treat people the same way you want to be treated that is my motto." she carelessly replied and a smile painted on her face.

"Aren't afraid of being used by bad people?" I asked her and my conscious kept on repeating bad people like me?

"I am but what can I do?" she replied as if she was doomed to be a goody two shoes forever

"When will I see you again?" I questioned and for an odd reason the idea of seeing her soon made me smile. Maybe I will gain a friend at the end of this plan?

"About that Rose is coming back from her honeymoon in two days and I don't won't her to think that something is going on between us. So this might be the first and last time we hangout." Maya explained as she stopped walking

"But Rose cannot control you and she is married so she won't care about me..." I replied but deep down I knew that it is a total lie: Rose still cares about me and I am going to win her back.

"My friendship with her is way too precious to lose for a guy so as I said before I can recommend you some other people to be friend." Maya suggested but her dark orbs kind of hid a unread feeling in them.

"As I said before I want you." I repeated

"Sorry Ian but I truly cannot be your friend." she refused yet again and before I can try to convince her, someone called her phone.

"Sorry." she said as she picked it up, answered and started walking to her car. But I won't let her go without convincing her and that's why I started following her.

"Mom come on! I am not ready! ....no!...no!....then I will happily die alone." she replied and let a loud groan out.

"What's wrong?" I asked and found myself really caring and wanting to know what's wrong with her.

"I have a blind date tomorrow." She announced as she stopped in front of a black range rover evoque.

"Don't go" the words yet again rushed out of my mouth and they surprised me more than her

"I have too." she sadly smiled as she opened the door of her car

"What if you lie and tell her that you are already dating someone?" I proposed as my hand shot to stop her from climbing to the driver's seat

"My mum will know. She will ask to meet him and I will get into trouble for lying." she refused and for some reason the wheels inside my head started turning. I need an idea or I will lose Maya too . What the hell! I mean I will not be able to use her for my plan in making Rose jealous.

"I can pose as your boyfriend." I offered again knowing that way both of us will benefit from such a play.

"Thanks for the offer but as i told you before I cannot do that to Rose." she smiled at me and withdrew her hand out of my grip and I was let to feel hopeless as she climbed into her car waved a goodbye then started to drive away.

Contents

Prologue

I knew that my cousin loved Ian forever.

He adored her too and promised her a forever.

Yet she grew tired of their on and off long distance love.

She gave up on him because of his player attitude and started a new relation with another man.

She wanted a fresh start and her now husband gave her all the love that she deserved.

I met Ian again when my cousin invited him for her wedding.

He sat beside me and I swear that his tears were nearly falling.

And to distract himself he grabbed a seat and started chatting to me.

His ex-lover's best friend. The girl he never paid attention to. The girl that was left pleasantly surprised that night thinking that she gained a friend.

Wedding bells and the Player

Maya's Pov:

Here, am I sitting in my cousin/best friend's wedding. I was the maid of honor. I am supposed to be the happiest hearing the ringing bells of Rose's wedding. But somehow they sounded more like a ticking clock and all that played in my mind was the same sickening idea: you are next. They are going to try their best to get you a husband soon.

I knew that my mum and aunts meant well but my heart pained at such an idea. I hated arranged marriages and fought against such an idea since I was young. But now since I am turning 24 and I am still single they decided to take control over my life and set me with who they believed to be the perfect fit.

They did that to Rose. But to be honest, she asked them to do so. She was so in love before. Yet the man she loved was a player and a manwhore. He toyed her for years and kept on promising her a happily ever after while he cheated and partied hard. He, Ian, swears still that she was his one and only.

He confessed for years that she was his first and last love. However, since he lived in another state, he cheated a lot and was open about it. Whenever she confronted him, he said that he was having some fun and she just needs to wait for him to be ready to be tied down in a real relation. And she waited. Rose waited for 10 freaking years because he was her high school crush and even when he moved away she kept on being faithful to him until her 25 birthday came. That's when she decided that she needed a radical change.

She, Rose, my cousin/sister/best friend was one year older than me and we surprised her with a huge surprise 25 birthday party, she surprised us all with a request. She asked my aunt/ her mum to set her on a date and my aunt couldn't be happier. Literally, my aunt was waiting for such a moment because she knew of the unhealthy and secret relation between Rose and Ian. My aunt in a matter of days sat rose in a blind date with Jacob and they kind of clicked. Rose became happy. She liked Jacob a lot and he made her forget about Ian. She was honest with Jacob and told him that she was broken and he promised to fix her back and he did.

There, they now smiling at each other and falling in love again after being lawfully tied to each other. The hope that glowed from both of them made me smile. Maybe it won't be that bad if my mum sets me with a guy? Maybe I will find my own Jacob?

"Is this seat taken?" the smooth manly voice came in a sort of hush and disturbed my thoughts I was about to lie and say yes but the man rudely sat before I could answer.

I looked at my right and as soon as I saw him, I was shocked. There was Ian , the ex-love interest of the new bride. I knew that Rose invited him but we doubted that his acceptance. Ian's muscled figure sat rigidly beside me and ignored my glare. His chocolate eyes were dark and fixed on Rose. Yet the latter was oblivious to his stare. She was so absorbed in a Jacob's story to notice anyone. Ian's eyes held troubled emotions and it might e my imagination but I could swear that they also held some hidden tears.

"She looks beautiful." he commented while still studying Rose who by notice him and offered him a small wave.

I just nodded . I didn't know if I was supposed to answer him or not. I didn't know how to act around him or why did he even sit beside me. I diverted my eyes away from him and started to pray for him to ignore me for the rest of the night but my prayers were soon disturbed yet again by him.

"You lost weight." he commented and for the first time since I knew him his eyes traveled up and down studying me. Don't get me wrong I knew him since I was young but he never cared to start a conversation with me unless it was about Rose. All his acknowledgements toward me were mere nods or greetings and that's it. I didn't care back then because I believed that he was so in love with Rose to the point of not caring about anyone and that made me happy. I was happy for Rose and now I was uncomfortable under Ian's gaze.

"Are you going to stay silent all night?" He questioned and I was debating if I should just nod and ignore him

"Why are you here?" the words flew out of my mouth before I could stop them. I didn't mean for them to sound harsh too but that question was all I could think about.

"I was invited." He firmly said but a small smile of acknowledgement showed on his face.

"I know." I replied while other questions started to pop in my head; why didn't you stop her? why didn't you fight for her? Didn't you say that she was your one and only then why did you allow her to fall out of your love?

"I don't know why am I here." Ian confessed as he fixed his glare again on the new married couple

"You flew for 3 hours but you don't know why?" I doubted his words and my eyes yet again traveled to study him: he was wearing a black suit and it was clearly made for him. It fitted his body perfectly and showed how fit he was. Ian always looked like a Greek god but his player like personality ruined the perfect picture of him. His face held discomfort as I questioned him and I debated if I am stepping out of my boundaries or not. He was a total stranger and here I was questioning his real intentions.

"I moved back here months ago." he informed me and I was shocked. He lives here now. He moved back but didn't contact the love of his life?

"Why didn't you stop her?" I finally had the guts to ask and his gaze once again traveled to me and connected with my dark orbs. I felt his discomfort but for some reason in mere second it all vanished as he sighed deeply but never looked away.

"She sounded happier and wasn't fazed when she called to invite me" he answered and his features darkened again.

"She is." I hushed afraid that my conformation will make him angrier

"I lost her." he confessed but sounded regretful and doubtful?

"sorry" I replied and for some reason I wanted to comfort him but I shook that thought away and focused on my glass of water.

"You still don't drink?" Ian' question came more as an exclamation and shock

"I don't." I just informed him and once again his gaze studied me as if I was some kind of an extraterrestrial creature

"Can you go with me to congratulate them?" Ian begged and I didn't want to. I didn't like the idea of being in awkward situations let alone a watcher of a love triangle.

"Can't you go alone?" I pleaded back

"Come on please May." he begged yet again

"But..." I tried to argue and at this Ian's hand shot and held mine as he begged for the third time. I didn't know what he said or whatever the arguments he used were because as soon as his hand connected with mine I felt a rush of electricity running down my spine. I tried to deny the feeling but It only grew fiercer as my searching eyes connected yet again with his. He was still rumbling. He was unfazed but the warmth that our hands produced and that made me believe that he didn't feel a thing. Maybe I was just hallucinating. All these preparations and talks about the wedding might made me softer, maybe they affected my mind. Ian cannot have an effect on me because he is a player and I hate that, because he is my best friend's ex-lover, because he was simply in love with Rose and will never notice me. I repressed all those strange shocking feelings away and decided on what am I going to do.

"Maya." I uttered surprising Ian

"What?" he didn't understand my latter word.

"My name is Maya and not May." I explained as I withdrew my hand from his grip...Our hands fit....Dammit I need to focus! he is a player and a manwhore! He is Rose's!

"Okay but Maya please don't let me talk to them alone?" he childishly and annoyingly begged again and again

"Okay but if you make it awkward I will simply walk away." I threatened and he shot me a winning smile.

As soon as he got up I mimicked. Then, to surprise me more his hand came into contact with my bare back. My flowing black dress was lengthy and cute but the only down side to it was that it was backless. I didn't care before but now the same unwanted tingles shot in my back and I was left to angrily wander.

"Your hand!" I angrily hushed at Ian not want to attract any attention

"What?" he was once again lost.

"Remove your hand." I ordered in a hush with the same angry tune.

"It is kind of a reflex sorry." Ian apologizes as he moved his hand but he didn't sound sincere at all.

We walked silently and I was debating my sanity all the way to the happily married couple's table. I didn't say a word to Ian as the idea of the tingles and who he is made me angrier by the minute. I should be hating him and not distracted by him!

"Ian you came." Rose greeted but sounded fake. Her gaze held some hidden indescribable feelings that made me feel uncomfortable.

"I had to say congrats to you and your husband." Ian sounded normal to anyone but I somehow pick up his anger

"Thank you for coming." Jacob and Rose said at the same time and then lovingly looked at each other

"204" they yelled cutely

"Huh?" Ian and I had the same reaction

"Your congratulation is the congrats number 204 that we heard today." they laughed at some kind of shared memory and Ian and I just nodded and walked away.

"Is that true love?" Ian asked hushing as if to himself

"What?" I asked to check if I was meant to answer

"That, them, the care, the smiles, the chemistry, the gazes and saying the same things at the same time?" Ian undoubtedly now questioned me

"I don't know." I answered frankly and he just nodded his head

"See you around town?" Ian asked as we reached our old table

"You are going to go already?" I for some reason wanted him to stay but shock that idea away

"Yeah I had enough of all this lovey dovey atmosphere." he answered honestly

"Me too" I hushed under my breaths

"Do you want me to drive you home?" Ian offered and I was shocked because he was never this nice to me.

"No thanks." I denied hating the idea of feeling any tingles or warmth caused by being near him

"I am just trying to gain a friend here." Ian confessed and I nearly choked on the water I was sipping

"Why? you never wanted to be friends back when we were younger." I daringly questioned

"Well now I want to and since I moved back here I never found time to explore the novelties around town so if is it okay with you can we meet somewhere and you can talk to me about all the new locations and news?" Ian asked and my head nodded on its own as if some foreign power controlled it.

"cool, give me your phone so I can give you my number." he ordered and I found myself obeying after all I just accepted.

Handing him my phone, I made sure that our hands won't touch. I tried to ignore the smile that drew on his face when he asked for my password and I refused to tell him so he started annoying me until I kind of yelled "Chains" and he looked at me in a funny way.

"So you like chains?" he asked with an evil smirk and i didn't get why

"Yes I do." I affirmed because for the moment I loved Nick Jonas's song Chains

"You are in rough stuff, I would have never guessed." Ian muffled a clear laugh and winked at me and that what it took me to get his dirty idea and my face heated immediately.

"Ian! I meant the song!" I yelled not caring about anyone's attention now and that's when Ian started to laugh uncontrollably.

"I know, I know..." Ian replied after laughing for nearly five minutes and then continued to open my phone and exchange our numbers.

"Here Miss pure." Ian handed me back my phone

"Miss pure?" I questioned him

"You are as pure as you were ten years ago. So yeah I saved your number under the name "Miss pure". It fits you." Ian explained offering me a smile and I just nodded

"So see you soon?" he questioned and I nodded again

"You know that a yes won't take that much effort." he teased and I just nodded and he shook his head as he walked away yelling see you soon miss pure

Ian's Pov

I felt Rose's gaze on us the whole time. Even if she played the part of the perfect bride she still holds some emotions for me and I know it and that's why I kept on talking to Maya. Don't get me wrong the latter is fun and easy to talk to and I hate to admit it but her purity kind of calms me down and makes me smile but Rose should e mine and if jealousy the game that she wants to play then I am ready to fire back.

I will get Rose back sooner or later!

I am sure that my friendship and innocent flirting with Maya will cause Rose to flip and confess that she will always love me and just me.

Please Vote and comment

and thanks for reading this first chapter

Hope that you like it

In between the missed friend &the not so broken guy

S econd chapter today :D

Vote & comment & thank for your reads and support

Maya's Pov:

"Hey!" I screamed happily as I answered my phone. I didn't talk to Rose since her wedding and it's been two weeks. Jacob and her went on a their honeymoon right away and I didn't want to disturb their romantic get away with my nonsense.

"I miss you so much." Rose replied immediately with the same cheerful attitude

"Same here, how are you and Jacob?" I questioned even though I saw their romantic posts on Facebook,twitter and Instagram

"We are amazing, the honeymoon is amazing and the wedding was beautiful." she cheered again and I could sense that she was truly happy

"The wedding was amazing." I agreed yet at the mention of such occasion an image of Ian in a black suit popped into my mind and I tried my best to ignore it.

"You seemed to have fun with Ian, all eyes were on your little friendly banter." Rose replied and her tone became a little colder. Am I not allowed to talk to Ian? Does she still hold feelings for him? and what about her husband, Jacob?

" He was being...well he was being Ian." I felt so awkward informing Rose about Ian. I felt like I was cheating on my friendship with her. I felt bad even though I didn't do a thing. Maybe I feel bad because of that shocking electric feeling I had when he held my hand maybe....

"You hated his personality before" her simple words troubled me and I didn't know if they were accusations of me breaking the girl code or mere observations

"He started talking to me..." I tried to assure her that I didn't do anything wrong

"Just be careful around him. He is a heart breaker." her tone and intention again weren't clear as her voice turned as cold as ever

"I am not falling for him." I announced in a praying tone as I remembered all the tingles and warmth his hand caused as his skin connected with mine

"I just don't want you to get hurt." Rose's tone was now back to her usual caring and friendly nature.

"I know...now tell me when are planing on coming back?" I decided to change the topic because Ian shouldn't matter to me. He didn't even contact me since the wedding. I knew that his overly friendly attitude was just fake.

Rose and I continued to chat for an hour until Jacob finally woke up and they had to go to have their breakfast. It was a regular Sunday for me so I planed to do the usual: lay down on my comfortable couch and watch a movie or two or three...As I started to look for some new Rom/com movies my ringtone "Chains" started to play.

That song now reminds me of Ian, I need to change it.

"hello?" i questioned answering without checking who is calling me

"Hi" a man's husky smooth voice answered back

" Who is this?" the voice sounded so familiar yet since my attention was diverted to reading one of the movie's summaries I couldn't know exactly who was calling me.

"You already forgot about me, Miss pure?" that stupid nickname echoed in my head and an image of a smirking Ian painted in my mind.

"Ian, what do you want?" I tried to play it cool and ignore my racing heart beat and guilty thoughts. He is Rose's my consciousness yelled at me.

"A date." He said it so simply yet that word made my world stop spinning, what the hell is wrong with him? why is he asking me for a date? didn't he know that it is against all rules of friendship?

"Sorry but I have to refuse." My heart pounded painfully for some reason but I ignored it. For Rose, I argued trying to calm my now racing heart.

"This is a first" he hushed as if to himself

"Sorry Ian." I apologizes but deep down I kept on question why does a stranger has such an effect on me? why can he pull all the right strings and make my heart race like no other?

"What about lunch just as friends." he offered again

"sorry but..." my words were cut by a deep sigh of his

"Come on May. You just turned me down twice in one minute and I was never turned down." he pleaded again

"If I say yes will you tell me the real reason behind this sudden friendly attitude?" I dared him because deep down my guts were telling me that even he was hiding something

"I am a man with a broken heart. I am trying to find a shoulder to lean on as I mend my heart. And I remember Rose talking about how you supported her for years, how you are the best friend that a man can ask for and how you helped her through the heart breaks I caused. I just need a friend." Ian completed his speech and now it was my turn to let out a sigh

"Rose told me to stay away from you." I confessed

"She doesn't trust me anymore but I assure that I have no hidden motives. Just a friendly lunch. Please?" Ian begged yet again

"We will have nothing to talk about." I tried to convince him of forgetting about lunch

"You don't know that." he insisted

"We don't know each other." I tried again

"Rose told me everything about you and I still remember some things about you." he argued stubbornly.

"I changed." I declared

"Then let me see how. Even though I am sure that you are still the same." Ian confidently announced

"You didn't knew me back when we were little." I accused him of lying

"Then let me get a chance to know the real you." Ian offered for the hundredth time

"Ian, sorry but I need to go." I gave up on trying to convincing him

"It is either you go out with me or I will come over." Ian rushed to say before I tipped to end called icon

"You know where I live? how?" I surprisingly questioned

"I have my way and you ,Miss pure, you have two hours to get ready and meet me at the french restaurant "Chez Balzac" He amusingly threatened

"No buts and sorry but now I have to go." he repeated my same line and ended the phone call letting me to groan loudly.

"I hate you Ian Mathews." I yelled letting some of my frustration out as one question controlled my thoughts why me?

Ian's Pov

She wasn't happy about this date and neither was I. But if I wanted my plan to work then I need her to go out with me or even fall for me so Rose can get blindly jealous and confess about her undying love for me. I needed to use Maya but she is making it so hard. I was never turned down by a girl but she turned me at least ten times in one conversation. She may mean nothing to me but her words kind of hurt my ego? Am I that bad? It is true, I am using her for my own good but it for the sake of Rose and I. Maya will understand when the plan is reviled. She will be happy for me and Rose. I am sure of that.

Now I have two hours to spare as I wait for my date with Maya. I know that it is going to be awkward but if she is as fun and out going as Rose described it will be all good. I mean back at the wedding her guards were up and she talked shortly but her presence kind of comforted me. Her eyes unexpectedly eased my anger. And her pure and innocent rumble and blush made me smile and laugh...I wonder if her password is still the same?

I shook my head clearing it from all images of Maya and now I had to focus on my one and ultimate goal getting Rose back.

As I Said Before I Want You!

Ian's Pov :

Am I being stood up? Should I call her? Did she figure out my real intentions?

These questions kept on replaying in my mind as I waited for Maya. She is late, way too late. I have been waiting for her for half an hour. People in the restaurant kept looking at me with sympathy as if they thought that my "date" forgot about me. I felt so awkward. Is this Karma? Is the universe making me pay for all the girls that I stood up?

Should I ring her? or Just go to her house?

As I stood up, I heard my name being called and there she stood. Maya was dressed simply and she looked so delicate. My eyes roam her body studying and I noticed how she shifted her weight from one leg to another to show her discomfort. She is nothing like the girls I dated. She is nothing like the girl I love, Rose. Maya was simple. She didn't dress glamorously. She since the age of four hated attention and since her discomfort was clear, I knew for sure that she still hates it.

"Ian?" she repeated as I didn't respond to her but kept on eyeing all her small details. She is a girl and I am a player so my reaction to her appearance is totally normal no one needs to read much into it. As soon as my eyes reached her face, I saw smooth skin uncovered by makeup, plump lips coated in light pink gloss and then dark orbs that showed clear discomfort and that was enough to shake out of my trance.

"You are late." I blamed as I took my seat back

"I didn't want to come" she bluntly confessed which shocked me but also made me chuckle. She is as blunt as a kid.

"And why is that? Am I not charming enough for you Miss pure? Or is your boyfriend possessive of you?" I teased her as she took her own seat and my eyes yet again traveled to study her plump lips and curvy figure.

"Honestly, I don't get why you want to be friend me and Ian both of us know that you are not as charming as people think. You are just a typical player." she again spoke freely not caring about my reaction and my smirk was flipped upside down because right at moment I knew that getting her under my charm won't be that easy. This girl can certainly read me like an open book.

"I told you my reason. Rose, the person I trust the most said that you are the greatest friend there is." I tired to convince her of my not so real intentions even though Rose did really tell me about Maya and how great she is.

"I can recommend some other friends for you." Maya shot back while a small smile took over her lips.

"I want you." I insisted and her eyes rapidly met mine. Her intense gaze made me shiver. I wanted to break our gaze but somehow her eyes hypnotized mine and kept them in chained.

"Salut et Bienvenue chez "Chez Balzac". Je suis Bryan et je suis votre serveur. Voila les menus et je reviendrai en quelques minutes pour prendre vos commandes." A voice came from beside and shook me back to sanity.

I looked at the waiter to thank him but found that his eyes were sat on Maya. He didn't pay attention to me even when I thanked him but when Maya did he gave her in flirting smile. I felt uneasy watching such scene but decided to ignore it. Maya , on the other hand seemed clueless to the man who was eyeing her. Even when she thanked him, her eyes never left the tablecloth.

"He was flirting with you." I stated with a kind of a not so understandable hostility

"No he wasn't. Not all men are players, you know?" Maya replied shacking her head like a kid and that made me smile.

"But what if he was, will you give him a chance of a date?" I tried to convince her

"That's my business." She tried to sound rude but failed. It is simply not her nature.

"Come on May, are you afraid to answer a little question?" I teased her hoping for an answer.

"No I am not and just so you know I don't like the idea of dating strangers. If I truly knew his personality and found it intriguing then yes. I mean the guy looks good but that can't be enough." Maya explained as she eyed the waiter and I feared that he will get the wrong signals from her so I cleared my throat to get her attention.

"So what are you going to order?" I asked trying to start a normal conversation where we both stay civil.

"I would rather eat at Chipotle." Maya mumbled to herself but I heard her

"Not into fancy food?" I teased her but was also surprise because I am used to girls loving fancy restaurants.

"Not into fancy things in general. You know that the price of such meals can provide all week meals for a poor family?" Maya informed in a blaming way and her eyes once again connected with mine but were shooting me a look of blame.

"I do charity." I announced hating her blaming glare

"If you eat regularly here, then you are not doing enough for charity."She judged but why are her words affecting me so deeply?

"I will I promise." my words escaped my mouth and I nearly regretted them but when Maya smile sweetly at me I couldn't help but smile

"You are not so bad you know?" Maya continued to speak as she read the menu again but I saw her cheeks turn a bit pink, Is she blushing?

"Is that a compliment ?" I teased her more loving the effect I had on her and that's when the waiter decided to interrupt us.

"Vous avez choisi?" he questioned in a fake french accent and I found myself getting irritated with him

"Yes!" I replied rudely and continued to order what I wanted

"And you mademoiselle?" he turned back his attention to Maya as he finished taking my order and she replied nicely to him. Our lunch was served rapidly and we kept silent as we ate. Maya wasn't like the girls I dated, she didn't talk unless someone addressed her and I was a bit frustrated with her. How am I going to get close to her if she is not allowing me? How am I going to use her to get Rose jealous if she is not caring about me at all.

"What's wrong?" I asked as her eyes nearly popped in shock as she looked at her desert

"You were right!" she exclaimed holding a small paper and giving it to me.

I took the paper rapidly and found a neat written sentence in it "If your date goes wrong call me :(number). I don't know why but for a freaking unknown reason I wanted to punch that waiter. He thought that we were on a date but had the rudeness and audacity to openly flirt with Maya? I crumbled the paper and tossed in my water glass.

"That's unnecessary." Maya hushed

"He is rude and what did you want to call him?" I sounded angrier than needed but honestly I didn't care because maybe this kind of anger will be understood as possessiveness

" No but you could act more civilly. He was honest about his feelings so why disrespect him by showing him that his emotions are worthless...." she continued to argue but I didn't care and just shot a warning glare at the waiter.

"He asked not because of feelings but because of your look. He kept eyeing you since he laid his eyes on you." I tried to convince her but she just shook her head and refused to believe me.

Desert went as silent as lunch. We didn't talk and the only argument we had after that was about payment. Maya refused to let me pay for her and she stubbornly paid for herself and left a tip for Bryan. She even shot an apologetic smile to him as we went out.

"You are a real goody two shoes" I teased as we went out to the parking lot

"Treat people the same way you want to be treated that is my motto." she carelessly replied and a smile painted on her face.

"Aren't afraid of being used by bad people?" I asked her and my conscious kept on repeating bad people like me?

"I am but what can I do?" she replied as if she was doomed to be a goody two shoes forever

"When will I see you again?" I questioned and for an odd reason the idea of seeing her soon made me smile. Maybe I will gain a friend at the end of this plan?

"About that Rose is coming back from her honeymoon in two days and I don't won't her to think that something is going on between us. So this might be the first and last time we hangout." Maya explained as she stopped walking

"But Rose cannot control you and she is married so she won't care about me..." I replied but deep down I knew that it is a total lie: Rose still cares about me and I am going to win her back.

"My friendship with her is way too precious to lose for a guy so as I said before I can recommend you some other people to be friend." Maya suggested but her dark orbs kind of hid a unread feeling in them.

"As I said before I want you." I repeated

"Sorry Ian but I truly cannot be your friend." she refused yet again and before I can try to convince her, someone called her phone.

"Sorry." she said as she picked it up, answered and started walking to her car. But I won't let her go without convincing her and that's why I started following her.

"Mom come on! I am not ready! ....no!...no!....then I will happily die alone." she replied and let a loud groan out.

"What's wrong?" I asked and found myself really caring and wanting to know what's wrong with her.

"I have a blind date tomorrow." She announced as she stopped in front of a black range rover evoque.

"Don't go" the words yet again rushed out of my mouth and they surprised me more than her

"I have too." she sadly smiled as she opened the door of her car

"What if you lie and tell her that you are already dating someone?" I proposed as my hand shot to stop her from climbing to the driver's seat

"My mum will know. She will ask to meet him and I will get into trouble for lying." she refused and for some reason the wheels inside my head started turning. I need an idea or I will lose Maya too . What the hell! I mean I will not be able to use her for my plan in making Rose jealous.

"I can pose as your boyfriend." I offered again knowing that way both of us will benefit from such a play.

"Thanks for the offer but as i told you before I cannot do that to Rose." she smiled at me and withdrew her hand out of my grip and I was let to feel hopeless as she climbed into her car waved a goodbye then started to drive away.

Drive Me Home

Ian's Pov

As soon as I woke up, I decided to see the new Instagram posts of Rose. Maya said that the latter will be coming home tomorrow and I couldn't wait to see her again. Yet my alibi to be around Rose was Maya and that won't work now because the latter is going on a blind date tonight. I felt irritated with such a thought because it shut down my plan before it even started.

From sickly watching the lovey dovey pictures of Rose and her husband, I searched for Maya's account and not so surprisingly I found no account belonging to her. How can a twenty first century girl live without an Instagram. Get frustrated with the idea of Maya always being unreachable, I tried to look for her on twitter and Facebook and I found her accounts. I was following her but she wasn't. I followed her maybe four years ago when Rose and I got into a huge fight. I the same as now wanted to use Maya to solve the problem but I guess that she didn't like me that much to follow me back.

Her accounts were deserted since forever and all there were in them were mere quotes and a couple of pictures that Rose or other friends tagged her in. This girl is a real riddle. How am I going to get closer to her if have nothing but Rose's past words about her?

According to Rose, Maya was the sweetest most faithful friend ever. Also, Maya is a goody two shoes who believes in the goodness of human beings. But this so delicate nature of hers shouldn't trick you. She is a strong, rude when needed, blunt and independent. The last time Rose talked about Maya, she also told me that she became the personal assistance of some huge business man.

I guess that that's all the clues that I have about her.

After aimlessly searching for clues in Maya's accounts, I decided to continue my day. For some reason the idea of who is Maya became hunting and I needed to wipe it out of my mind by any means. I went to my own company that day and everything went so smoothly in mere months this company will be the talk of all the business market. It was growing steadily and rapidly and I am truly proud of it. My mind kept on drifting to same unanswered question " Who is Maya?" but every time it did I ignored it.

At nearly 9 pm, when I was driving myself home, my cell phone ringed and without caring about who it is I just put them on high speakers. A sniff that's all I heard and my heart started racing and my head filled with dark possibilities. Is she okay?

"Maya, what's wrong?" I rapidly questioned

"Ian can you please come pick me up?" She brokenly questioned

"Give me the address." I ordered and as soon as I got I drove literally like a mad man. Maya might be just an acquaintance of mine but her crying voice did things to me. I just didn't like seeing her broken.

As I drove by the famous Italian restaurant, her date location I guess, I found her standing near its door. She was dressed in this deep red dress, her black hair fell freely on her shoulders and she had a little bit of makeup. She hugged herself and seemed lost. I didn't like seeing her this way. The Maya that went out with me yesterday was fierce and full of life but this Maya looked broken.

"May..." I hushed as I got out of the car and walked to her

"Thank you so much for coming Ian. I didn't mean to trouble you but I didn't drive here and I wanted to call Rose but she is not here and...." she continued to ramble endlessly as she wiped her heavily falling tears.

"It is more than okay. But are you okay?" I questioned her and found myself wanting to hug her and protect her.

"Yes, now can you please drive me home?" she asked and I just obeyed.

She sat there silent for more than five minutes. Not a word erupted from her lips and I was left to wonder. She played with hem for her dress and sighed from time to time and I didn't know if I should voice my questions. I was no expert in girls emotions and drama so maybe staying silent would be the best.

"Dammit, May if you keep on crying and sighing at least tell me what's wrong?" I cracked under the haunting voices of her pain

"My blind date was my boss's son. At the beginning I was impressed by how nice he is. Then as we ate dinner he started sending me signals of him wanting to do things but I played it cool and ignored him..." she sniffed again as she explained and my knuckles tightened around the wheels

"What things?" I stupidly asked even though I knew exactly what she meant

"Things as in....things. But after dinner he shared his intentions either I sleep with him or he will get me fired." she disgustingly said as if remembering the scene

"That bastard and What did you say?" I replied as I found some kind of a foreign protectiveness over her.

"I need to find a job." Maya replied with a loud sigh

"Be my personal assistance. My company is growing and I need help around it." I offered and the idea excited me. That way Maya will benefit and I will make Rose jealous.

"Thank you Ian but I doubt that Rose will be okay with that." Maya offered me a smile as she refused

"Why is it always about her?" I asked seeing how selfless Maya was

"It is not about her. It is about my friendship with her. I won't risk it..." Maya again smiled and her phone ringed out of nowhere

"It is Rose. I have to pick up but please keep quite." she begged and I nodded

"Hey...I miss you too...No the date wasn't that great...He tried to get me too sleep with him...I lost my job too...He kind of put his hand too low and you know and while we were having dinner he ...you know." Maya explained and to Rose and she was speaking so uneasily but all the events that she reported angered me for a reason.

"Son of..." the words escaped my mouth as a loud growl and Maya's eyes doubled in size as her hand shot to my mouth's direction to shut it. her palm laid on my lips and all I could think of that moment was how smooth her skin was.

"I needed someone to drive me back and you weren't here. I don't know why Ian's name popped in my mind but at that time he sounded like my only solution. No him and I, we are not close. I am clearly not under his spell" Maya tried to argue endlessly with Rose and it made me smile to know that my plan is somehow working.

"Rose?" I called as I snatched Maya's phone out of her hand and put Rose on high speakers.

"Ian." Rose sounded annoyed as hell.

"Tell Maya that it is okay for her to be my personal assistance. I offered her the job but she wouldn't accept it because she is afraid that it will ruin your friendship. Are you okay with letting her be jobless, Rose?" I teased knowing that Rose will accept because these girls always looked up for each other.

"Maya do you want to work with him?" Rose asked

" I don't know. I could search for other options." Maya offered and I was once again struck by her selflessness

"Rose come on! you know that Maya needs this and I know that she will be a great help around the office so tell her to accept already." I nearly yelled at Rose

"Okay, okay but you won't start tomorrow! you have to pick me and Jacob from the airport at 9 am." Rose agreed and I was happy because my plan is going well.

Step one achieved!

"About that my car refused to start this morning. Maybe I just need to ask your mum or mine to pick you up." Maya sadly informed Rose

"We will pick you up tomorrow then head to the company." I offered and both girls went silent.

I need to be around Rose if I am going to make her jealous. I need to pamper Maya in front of her so her perfect happy wife facade will break. I need Rose to get as jealous as possible so she can acknowledge that she is still in love with me and not Jacob.

"Good night for now Rose." I said as I took charge of the situation and hangup on her

The ride after that went silent. Maya ignored my existence and seemed to be lost in deep thoughts. I drove her to her apartment and as soon as she felt my car stopping she opened her door and jumped out of it. I was expecting some kind of an acknowledgement after all I just offered her a job and saved her from walking home with tearful eyes. But nothing happened. She just picked her phone and jumped out of my car.

"Hey, did I do something wrong?" I yelled as I followed her to her doorstep

"No" she replied without looking at me and kept looking for her keys

"Then why didn't you thank me?" I sounded as whiny as a kid. What is this girl doing to me?

"I said thank you earlier. isn't that enough?" She asked as her orbs met mine. They were black and confused. Emotions stormed in them and I as always was held a slave to her gaze. I just couldn't look away.

"What's wrong May?" I simply questioned

"You. You are what's wrong. I don't know if I should trust you or run away and hide from you. You were never interested in knowing me as a friend but now you want to befriend me and to be my boss. I can't help but feel that you have an hidden motive behind such acts. Do you somehow want to get back to Rose by befriending me?" she asked as bluntly as always. It amazed me how she read my intentions so easily and at the same time I felt so low as i was caught red handed.

"I don't have motives. I just feel comfortable around you. You are honest, nice and independent. You care about humanity and goodness more than needed and you are smart and faithful and those are all the traits that I want in a friend and in an assistance." I explained to her and all but my first sentence were true. Maya's eyes studied me for some more time as if searching for any evidence to prove that all my speech was a lie but as I said before all my words were true.

"Thank you." she replied sounding happier and without a warning she hugged me. Her hands circled my neck as she thanked me again but I for a reason I froze under her touch. All I cared about was how she smelt so rosy and how her body perfectly fitted with mine. My hands in a minute reacted and hugged her closer. I felt a sense of comfort and completeness as held her. I never felt that way with any girl before even Rose. Maya's head laid exactly under my chin. She was taller than Rose. Perfectly tall to fit exactly under my chin.

"Ian? you can let go now." Maya's words echoed in my mind and I found myself reluctant to let her go but I guess that I needed to.

"Good night Ian." she said as I let her go and I swear I saw a hint of a blush on her cheeks. Such idea made me smile, for a reason.

"Goodnight May and be ready by 7:00 am tomorrow. We will have breakfast, pick up rose then go to the company. Okay?" I offered and she nodded while opening her door repeating a goodnight and closing the door behind her.

She fits perfectly against my body!

that idea haunted me even when I went to sleep but deep down I knew that I cannot try to have Maya as more than a friend and a fake love interest because anything else will ruin my chances at getting back with Rose my one and only true love.

I need to draw some boundaries between Maya and I! I need to keep things professional and flirty only when Rose is around.

Vote & comment & thank for your reads and support

What will happen NEXT?

Ian and Maya working together, how will that end up?

& Rose is back again, what drama and mixed feelings will erupt soon?

& thanks again <3 ^-^ *-*

You Are not Her Type

Maya's Pov:

I was woke up way too late. Ian said that he is going to pick me up by 7 am and here I was at waking up at 6:45 am. I rushed to the bathroom, washed my face, brushed my teeth and try to find a way to style my hair. As I completed my french braid, the door bell ringed.

"I am so sorry Ian. I don't know what happened by my alarm didn't go off...I don't know what's wrong with all the machines that own. Just give me 15 minutes and I will be ready. okay?" I continued to ramble but there was no answer.

I looked behind me and found that Ian was there but he was busy eyeing me up and down. His eyes traveled yet again studying all my curves. My pajama set wasn't revealing. It was simple just a short shorts and a big t-shirt. So he had nothing to look at but I guess that I was wrong because he continued to do the same action for a minute then kind of cleared his throat to end the silence that grew between us.

"It is okay May. Take your time." he replied as he scratched the back of his neck

"Okay, make yourself at home." I replied and went back to my bathroom

As I looked myself at the mirror when I ended putting on my outfit, I found a very normal girl. Nothing that Ian, the player and the Greek god should eye. I am too plain for his taste but why is he being nice to me? Why is he offering me this job and being near me wherever?

"I am ready to go and sorry for the worst first impression ever." I said as entered my living room and found Ian sitting on my couch with his phone in hand.

"It wasn't that bad." he smiled at me and now it was my turn to study his outfit and how it hugged his figure so perfectly.

Focus Maya! You cannot feel anything towards him because of Rose, because of his nature and because somehow his intentions are not totally proven true. So stay out of his reach and try to look away from him those tingly feelings won't erupt again.

"So where do you want to have breakfast?" Ian asked as he walked to me and started to name few locations

"Can't we have it here?" I offered and he just shook his head fiercely and in one swift move grabbed my hand in his and led the way! So far for not touching him and welcome to the tingles. Dear god why does he have such an effect on me. My skin burnt where his hand laid and I wand to pull my hand but feared of seeming rude to the man who is helping me.

"Come on, I will show you one of the places that I love most." Ian sounded like a kid but I couldn't help but love his enthusiasm

He drove us to this small coffee shop. It has a homey decor and the waiters there were so welcoming. The atmosphere felt perfect even for a girl that does not like to go out like me. When the menus came I ordered a black coffee and egg whites omelet . As our orders came, we kept some small talks going nothing much just questions about our favorite things.

"Why did you push the sugar away?" Ian questioned as he noticed my action

"Since I had to lose weight when I was a teen, I gave up sugar for good." I informed remembering how my body image still troubles me.

"You are curvy May. That's the nature of your body. And after all the weight you lost you truly look good so there is no need to torture yourself." Ian's words sounded sincere and I couldn't help but smile at him. He just said that I ,the girl who always lived in the shadows, looks good.

"Thank you but Ian we need to hurry up. the newly weds'plane will be here soon." I informed and he obeyed letting us silently eat.

"Rose!" I yelled as I ran to her and hugged her

"Maya" she mimicked

Ian's Pov

"Ian, right?" Jacob asked as we watched the girls hugging

"Yeah..." I didn't know why he was addressing me and wanted to ignore him but that will definitely blow my cover and show my jealousy.

"Thanks for picking us up. I know that this must be awkward for you after all Rose was your ex." He continued to speak not picking the glares I was sending him.

"I am doing it for Maya." I lied

"She is an amazing girl but I highly doubt that she will give you a chance..."
He confidently spoke on Maya's behalf and I found myself hating him
more

"And what gives you such an idea?" I dared him

"You are not the kind of guy she likes. Rose and I tried to set her up on blind
dates before and she gave us these certain characteristics and Rose told me
that they don't exist in you." He explained as the girls started walking to
us

"And what is her kind of guy?" I questioned and I really wanted to know.

"Ask her." Jacob continued as he himself went to hug Maya and the smile
that plastered on her face was bigger than ever.

"MayMay, we missed you." he teased her

"I missed both of you too Jack." Maya said as she side hugged both Jacob
and Rose

"We need to go guys. It is already late for us to go to work." I announced
stopping their cute moment

Jacob sat in the front seat as the girls wanted to chat and catch up. I was
irritated by his presence but some Maya's giggle was enough to ease me.
Rose was telling her stories and showing her pictures and Maya sounded
as happy as ever.

"We need to find you a boyfriend MayMay, or else your mum will bombard
you with different blind dates." Rose spoke and I couldn't help but look at
the rearview mirror to study Maya's reaction.

"I don't want to be in a relationship right now. I want to wait for the right
guy." she sounded as innocent and dreamy as a kid

"My offer still stands." my words got me the attention of all

"What offer?" Rose and Jacob questioned but why does the latter care! I mean Rose is Maya's best friend and my ex-lover so she should care but why does Jacob keeps on on interfering?

"I told her that I can act as her boyfriend in front of her mum and that way she won't need to go on blind dates." As I finished my words I continued on studying Rose's reaction her glare held mine in rearview mirror and some unresolved anger was wide and clear in her eyes.

Jealousy, I guess ! step two achieved!

"It might actually work." Rose said with mischief all over her face.

"No I cannot do that. Ian cannot fit the role. Mum will know the second she sees him and your mum already knows about your past." Maya denied and I felt the a foreign kind of pain in my chest.

"What is your type?" my question sounded more like a yell and that's when Maya's eyes connected with mine

"It does not matter Ian. It will never work." Maya tried to stubbornly dismiss me and I felt my anger raising so without giving a warning decided to park the car on the side of the road.

"Ian?" they all questioned but my eyes were on the same girl that turned me down endlessly

"What is so wrong about me? Why don't I fit your so called list? Am I that bad?" I didn't mean to yell at her but I couldn't suppress my anger. I was being nice to her. I was being caring and helpful so what does she need? I know that my intentions are evil but come on I am not that bad!

"Nothing is wrong with you Ian." Maya tried to sweetly assure but I wasn't convinced

"May!" I said in the same angry tone

"You let him call you May?" Rose interfered and sounded so surprised

"I tried to correct him but he ignored me." Maya rushed into telling Rose and while doing so she sounded as guilty as hell.

"May, I am still waiting for an answer." I repeated ignoring Rose and Jacob's questioning glares glares

"Can I start working tomorrow? I am not feeling good anymore. I will just walk home." Maya replied ignoring me yet again and my level of frustration reach its highest as she opened the door of the car, got out and started walking

"Why are you always running away from me?" I questioned and yelled at Maya as I ran behind her and caught her hand turning her around to face me.

"I am not trying to avoid you but I am trying to avoid hurting your feelings. When I said that you are not my type I meant it because I vowed to never date a guy like you. You drink a lot. You play around. You made rose cry for years. And if your offer still exist then I am going for you. I don't like to mix business and personal business so my type is basically anything but you. I was used to telling Rose that if both of you got married and had kids and I got married and had kids too I will never let our kids play together because I know for sure that your kids will be the same as you." Maya yelled at me and her frustration was now erupting too.

Her eyes looked teary and I wanted to hug. I was surprisingly not offended by her words but they kind of pained me. So I will never have a chance with Maya. Not even the fake relationship that I was hoping for. I was never rejected before yet here I am getting rejected and humiliated by an unnoticed girl, a girl who got my blood boiling and for some reason I lost all sanity pulled her closer to my body and connected our lips.

Vote & comment & thank for your reads and support

What will happen after the kiss?

Ian and Maya working together, will they still work together and how will that end up?

& Rose is back again, what drama and mixed feelings will erupt soon?

& thanks again <3 ^-^ *-*

Something Between An Acquaintance And A Friend

Maya's Pov :

How would you feel if a Greek god kissed you then mumbled the name of your best friend against your lips? How would you feel if the guy that you just started trusting and befriending turned out to be just a liar? How could I not cry my heart out after being used and manipulated?

After that passionate rough kiss, the only word that came out of Ian's mouth was Rose. He kissed me senseless and tingles shot all over my body but as soon as our lips parted my heart broke. He was thinking of her while kissing me. I knew that befriending me wasn't his real motive. I knew that he didn't care about me at all he was just using me.

I didn't know how but I escaped his arms and ran as fast as I could. He didn't follow me and I don't know what happened to Rose and Jacob and if Rose saw the kiss or not. I do not care anymore because I will certainly distance myself away from all of them. I needed an escape from that love triangle. I needed some distance from the man who so suddenly reappeared in my life ,ripped my heart and stepped on it without caring.

As I sat on my bed now, I can't but remember the feels of Ian's lips against mine, how he seemed so passionate about it as if his whole life depended on it. I tried to push him away at the very start but I couldn't resist for much time. His hand held me close and even air couldn't separate us. Our bodies melded together and passion flared between us. His tongue begged for entrance and I gave it to him. I never felt so safe and so complete before but between Ian's hands I couldn't care less about what was happening around us all that mattered back then was our racing heart beats,our connected lips and our bodies that fitted like a perfect puzzle.

My phone started ringing yet again and I knew who it was, it was Rose. I just betrayed her and literally kissed her ex in front of her without asking for her approval. I just broke a major rule in girl code. I didn't know if I should pick up or let her tenth phone call go to voice mail. My heart was torturing me and I couldn't but blame myself.

"Maya open up this stupid door. I am seriously jetlagged and don't have the power to stand her forever." Rose's yells surprised me and I no more can ignore her. I had to open up the door and let her that she doesn't trust me anymore.

"I am so sorry. I never meant to kiss him. It all happened too fast. I didn't start it but I couldn't push him away. I am the worst friend there is. I am so sorry Rose..." I said and all the sobs that tried to muffle before escaped my throat.

"I know that. Ian took the blame for the kiss he said that he forced himself on you and that's why you ran." Rose tried to comfort me but I knew deep down that enjoyed that sinful kiss. I was blamed for it as much as Ian was.

"I am so sorry Rose." I apologized again as I allowed her in my apartment.

"It is okay. Ian is a player by nature and that was meant to happen with you or with any other girl." she said so simply yet some pain was noticeable in her tone

"You still love him, don't you?" I asked and tried my best to cover up my disappointment

"I don't I can call my feelings for him as love anymore but I still feel things for him. To be honest, I don't know if I will ever stop feeling things for him. He has been there all my life you know? and I can't seem to forget about him totally." Rose confessed with a long sigh as she sat on couch

"What about Jacob?" I blurted out afraid that the little moment I shared with Ian could destroy their newly shared vows

"Jacob is my soulmate. He knows about the complicated feelings I hold Ian. He promised me that little by little he will erase them all. I cannot say that he succeeded in his mission by he is doing a great job. He is just amazing." Rose explained and I saw the same old sparkles shine in her eyes. I could truly see that she is in love with Jacob and that her emotions for the latter are getting stronger as days go by. Yet, when she also talked about Ian she had some sort of possessiveness in her words and that made me regret kissing him and feeling different about him.

"By the way Ian says sorry about the mistake of a kiss and that he still wants to be his assistance." Rose announced and my heart broke because he acknowledge our kiss as a mistake.

"Tell him that I am getting my old job back. My boss called. And when I told him about his son, he promised me to deal with him. If Nicolas tried to make any move on me his dad will not announce as the new CEO next month." I informed Rose and inside I was torn between feeling happy for having my old job back and being away from Ian and being sad and gloomy for the same reason.

"But Nicolas will still be working there, meeting him will be awkward and he may do stuff to you. Also, after a month no one will be stopping him from using the same threats." Rose sounded so concerned and I knew that she trusted me with Ian more than with Nicolas

"When that happens, I will deal with him. But for now I want to go back to my office. The company needs me and I can let down my boss, when he has so much to do before retiring." I insisted and Rose nodded in agreement.

"Maya, are you falling for Ian?" Rose questioned both took by surprise and echoed in mind repeatedly. I mean it makes sense; he makes me blush, I feel happily giddy between his arms and when he touches me or when he kissed me, I felt electrified and tingles rose all over my body...I am surly feeling something for him. But can I call such feeling love when I don't the real him?

"No..." I denied hoping that she won't read much into my shacking tone

"Okay then I have to go Jacob and I are going to have dinner with his family." Rose announced and I just nodded and bid her goodbye.

After Rose's visit my day was uneventful. I had nothing to do other than watching movies and series and trying hardly to erase any memory I had of Ian. The kiss replied in mind countless times and it frustrated me more and more. Am I really falling for the man who just broke my heart?

"Hello...." I picked up the phone yet again without reading the name of my caller

"May..." I froze as his rough troubled voice reached my ears.

"Yes?" I replied after a minute of arguing if I should just hangup on him or hear him out

"I am sorry. I shouldn't have kissed you. It was a mistake." he said and each word felt like a dagger stabbing my heart.

"I forgive you. I knew it from the start you were using me to get closer to Rose." I replied trying to act strong

"I never planned to kiss you. I just wanted to make her jealous..." he confessed and my tears silently fell

"It is okay but leave me out of your future plans. I believe in Rose and Jacob's love." I announced strictly not because I wanted Ian for myself but because I truly believe that Rose is in love with Jacob and that he is in love with her too.

"I am sorry but you should know that I love her." He sounded truthful and with that my heart finally shattered in pain

"I know. Is there anything else you want to say before I hangup?" I asked wanting him to deny and just allow us to part ways

"I don't want you to go back to your old company." Ian suddenly declared with a clear decisiveness.

" Sorry Ian but I have too." I said and I could swear that I heard him cursing for a reason

"You don't have to. I offered you a job and that Nicolas guy will try to get you in his bed again." Ian sounded so frustrated as he argued with me.

"He won't and thank you for the proposal but I have to decline." I tried to sound as professional and confident as possible.

"How do you know that?" He dared and nearly yelled

"Why do you care?" I yelled back at him

"Because we are friends!" Ian defended and that is when my door bell ringed

"Ian wait there is someone at the door." I informed him and got up with the phone still in my hand listening to Ian nagging endlessly about Nicolas and how inappropriate it will be to work with a boss who wanted to have a physical relationship with me. Did he forget about our kiss? wasn't that physical something? or is it mere nothing to him?

"Nicolas?" I questioned as I opened the door and saw my boss's son standing with a bouquet of roses in his hand.

" Maya, I came to say sorry." he sounded regretful and honest

"Thank you...." I didn't know how to act around him since the last time I met him he made it so awkward.

"Can we start over?" he questioned with a hopeful smile as he handed me the flowers.

"No." Ian yelled through the phone which reminded me that he is still on the phone.

"I think that there is no harm in starting over, but if you try anything. I promise you that you will never have your dad's company." I shot him a daring glare and ignored Ian who was rambling nonsense about how stupid I am for giving Nicolas a chance.

"I promise that I have no bad intentions whatsoever. I am here to redeem myself and I am doing it not for the company or for my dad. I am doing it because after seeing how my dad talks about you like a daughter and how he respects you so much, I realized that I made a huge mistake. You are not the kind of girl to have one nightstands. You are innocent." Nicholas continued his speech with lopsided grin that made him look cute and couldn't help but chuckle

"May?" I forgot about Ian again and I could totally feel that his tone changed and was urging me to acknowledge him, but why should I?

"Sorry, Ian but I have a guest right. So if there is nothing urgent I would like to hangup." I firmly said as I ushered Nicholas to get in.

"Why are you doing this May? He tried to use you the first time so why are you inviting him in?" Ian sounded angrier than ever but why should I care when he just broke my heart to pieces?

"Why am I talking to you right now? and Why are you still calling me your friend when you obviously used me too?" I questioned with all the anger that I could manage and then hang up before getting an answer.

"So, is that a boyfriend or an ex?" Nicholas asked as he sat on the couch

"Neither." I corrected him

"But his yells were so loud. He is jealous and protective." Nicholas tried to explain his former assumption

"He is something between an acquaintance and a friend." I tried to explain to Nicholas

"He surely didn't sound like that." Nicholas teased again and I saw the playful look that he had

"So coffee or tea?" I tried to change the subject

"coffee for sure." Nicholas said as he picked up the remote and shook in his hand to prove that he is turning on the TV and i laughed at how comfortable he is in a stranger's house.

"So what are we watching ?" I asked as I handed him his cup of coffee

"Nothing is good to watch. What do you think of playing twenty questions?" Nicholas asked and I smiled at him and nodded but my phone buzzed announcing a that I received a text.

"If he tried anything this time. I am going to kill him. Ian" Who does he think he is?

"There is no need. We are friends now." I sent back and smiled back at Nicholas

"First rule you have to call me nick." Nicholas said with a childish grin

"Never heard of such rule in twenty questions." I teased him a bit and his smile grew wider

"come on Yaya. Let's start the game." he teased back and laughed at my new nickname

"Yaya? really how childish can that be?" I playfully mocked him and suddenly it was like this was my first meeting with Nicholas. I forgot all about the date and enjoyed the real him. I wish he acted this way on the date, maybe I wouldn't have kissed Ian if Nicholas acted this way on our date....Ian dear god how could he keep on popping in my mind endlessly.

"I like that nickname." Nick answered back with the same grin

"I like it too now let's play." I said and he nodded and started asking me about my favorite things.

Vote & comment & thank for your reads and support

What will happen next? Maya and Nick do you ship them?

Lunch and Yaya

Ian's Pov:

I am having lunch with Rose. I couldn't believe that the latter accepted my invitation but surprisingly she did. I said that I missed the old times and she agreed to meet up with me. I knew that she informed Jacob about our plans. I knew that he had a say in us meeting . That irritated me a lot but he allowed her and that made me the happiest. That stupid guy trusted me with her and allowed her to maybe connect with me again and even fall in love.

I decided to wait for Rose in front of the restaurant that picked. I am going to be a total gentleman to her. I will open the door for her, help her to sit on her chair and pay the bill for sure. I will be the perfect prince and that way her feelings for me will ignite again and hopefully she will dump Jacob and run to my hands.

"Hey." she saluted me with her usual smile

"Hi." I greeted her back and looked deeply in her blue orbs. The same eyes that I loved for years. The same ocean eyes that charmed me and put me under a spell.

"Shall we go in?" she questioned and I nodded then walked with her.

As planned, I acted as the perfect gentleman. I made her laugh and giggle and those sounds were pure music to my ears. I am truly in love with this woman. Rose kept on talking endlessly about her adventures with Jacob and even if that tortured me on the inside I smiled and kept a friendly facade for her. Be a prince charming and maybe she will fall for you again!

As I agreed on playing it cool, her phone beeped announcing a text and she excused herself to read it. After seconds the smile on her face grew wider. She chuckled silently and I wanted to know what Jacob could have said to earn such a smile from her.

"Jacob?" I asked intruding but I didn't really care

"Maya." Rose corrected and my heart fastened rapidly at the mention of Maya's name.

"Is she okay?" I felt all my cold facade and high walls trembling and break-ing. Why do I care about Maya or her well being?

"She is great. I didn't meet her since the incident between you too but we have been texting." Rose declared as she once again chuckled at what Maya sent her.

"So it is been a whole week? She is that busy?" I questioned yet again and found my questions unreasonable. Why do I care? Maybe because I knew that Maya and Rose couldn't stay apart from each other for more than a day. Yeah my care is just out of friendship.

"Nick and Maya have been working on a secret project and while doing so they have be pranking each other and all. They grew close and are becoming inseparable. Maya send me their updates everyday." Rose laughingly said as if visioning one of Maya's or Nicholas's pranks. But while I heard her words I felt a foreign pang of pain in my chest. Just like the day of that kiss, when she ran away, when Nicholas came to her and she invited him in, my heart raced in a painful way and then just seemed to abruptly stop.

"They are friends now?" the words escaped my mouth and wanted to take them back. Why I am sounding so vulnerable? Why do I seem to lose control when Maya is mentioned or is around?

"He calls her Yaya and his own best friend. He is getting possessive of her friendship and when he succeeds in keeping her away day and night he actually tease me for being her new best friend." Rose said playfully as she shook her head disagreeing

"Night?" that was all I heard. I don't know why but images of me and Maya kissing started to replay in my mind. I remembered how she felt against me, how she fitted like her body was made for mine, how she tasted and felt as I kissed her lips and how she reacted to me. Then suddenly the same image changed and there was Maya kissing another guy. Panting as he continues to kiss her senseless and smiling as he asks for entrance.

"Ian?" Rose questioned and I tried my best to focus on the woman that I love but those images of Maya kissing a stranger kept on haunting me.

"What were we talking about before Maya and Nicholas were mentioned?" I tried to change the subject hoping that Rose won't sense my discomfort.

"Are sure that you are okay?" She questioned and I nodded but images were haunting me and for a reason torturing me.

"What are you planing to do after lunch?" I asked wanting to focus on Rose again

"Jacob and I are getting formally introduced to Nicholas." Rose sounded cheerful at the idea but I didn't know which guy name tortured me more!

"Why such formalities?" I dared to ask because if he wasn't dating May then he shouldn't be introduced formally to her family and friends.

"Maya insisted on the need of us knowing the real him. Since she gave him a second chance, he proved himself trustworthy. We kept on doubting him and even speculating his every move but Maya promised us that he is one the greatest people she has ever met. She added him in a group discussion at first we resentfully talked to him but then we warmed up to him and started consider him as part of our group. Now Maya says that it is the right time to finally meet him in person." Rose explained and I now I can surely say that I hate Nicholas. I don't know why but he invaded the group's life easily. Yet when I tried to befriend Maya she rejected me countless times. Is he better than me? handsomer? richer? I am sure that Maya won't care about such titles but I can't help but wonder at how this idiot of a man put Maya under his spell in just a week while I was rejected all the time...

"You spacing out..." Rose indicated with a searching tone

"I am tired. The past few days were hectic." I lied but she seemed to believe it. She couldn't read me like an open book...not like Maya...

"Best of luck with your company." Rose wished and I smiled at her and thanked her then started to play with my meal as Rose silently ate. For an unknown reason I had lost my appetite to both eat and talk.

"Thanks for lunch, Ian." Rose thanked me as we went out and before she leaved she hugged me.

I was expecting sparks but all I felt was some warmth and familiarity. What is wrong with and why did my soul yearn for Rose to turn into Maya at that very second. Why did I wish to have Maya this close? Why did I wish to kiss her senseless again? Am I going insane?

Vote & comment & thank for your reads and support

What will happen next? Maya and Nick do you ship them?

We are friends you know?

Ian's Pov

In the last few days, my mourning routine changed. As soon as I wake up, I went online to discover Rose's new updates. Everything was normal, a lovey dovey quote on facebook were she tagged Jacob, few tweets on twitter and I guess a new pic on Instagram. Yet the picture wasn't so usual. The picture made my heart race painfully for a reason. I didn't know if it is because of the first couple or because of the second.

Rose's new Instagram picture was of her, Jacob, Maya and another guy, Nicholas, I guess.Rose was sitting pretty close to Jacob and he was smiling down at her and she returned the same loving smile. Then there was Maya in the background standing with Nicholas. They were standing close to each other and their eyes were twinkling in happiness. His hand rested on her upper arm and her cheeks looked rosier than normal. She was blushing. He made her blush. Rose posted the pic with hashtags welcoming Nicholas to the group and saying that he fitted right in.

My eyes kept on studying both woman then both men and anger rose in me. I knew that I will always be jealous over Rose but something ticked in me while I saw Maya with Nickolas. I don't know why but for the slightest moment I wished to be there , in his place. I wanted to be the cause of Maya's blush. I made her blush before and that was surprisingly rewarding. I felt happy when her cheeks painted in a deep shade of pink. I tried to shake those images away but they kept on haunting me. Maybe I miss Maya, after all I considered her as a friend and I have not seen her for the past two weeks.

Without thinking of what I am going to say or do, I just picked up the phone and dialed Maya's number. I don't know if she is going to pickup, hangup or let it go to her voicemail. My heart raced loudly as the beeps echoed in my ears and I suddenly became so self-conscious. Maya can reject my calls after all, I tricked her, played her, used her and forcefully kissed her...

"Hello?" a manly voice questioned and I froze. My blood started to unreasonably boil inside me as I heard him repeat his greetings over and over again. Why is he allowed to answer her calls? Why is she with him, when it is only eight in the morning? Are they a couple? Did he sleep with her?

"Where is Maya?" I sounded angry and mad but I didn't care anymore. Maybe I am trying to protect Maya from another heart break...Nicolas doesn't deserve her she is way too pure for him.

"Wait for a second." he informed me and continued to yell "Yaya, someone is calling you!" well if I wasn't irritated back then now I am surly

"Hey." her soothing voice reached my ears and I for a reason sighed in relief

"May." I uttered and the words literally failed me after so and I was left with a blank mind, why did I call her again?

"Ian? how are you?" she politely asked but her tone showed that she was alert and that my call was unexpected

"Good, how about you?" I questioned her back

"Great actually." she replied with an enthusiastic tone

"How is the old job treating you?" I asked but in reality I wanted to know how Nicholas was treating her and what is the nature of their relationship

"Well Nicholas became the CEO earlier than expected and since we became close, my old job became more fun." She sounded cheerful and I heard her giggle at something Nicholas did and that made my blood boil. I hate that man with a passion now. Don't ask me why because I don't clearly know but all that matters is that I hate him.

"cool." I replied shortly while trying to keep my tone neutral

"Did you need something?" Maya questioned me and I knew that her attention was not drawn to me but to the man who made her giggle

"No, I just wanted to check on you. We are friends you know?" I lamely argued but deep down this conversation kept on paining me more and more

"Yeah sure and thanks." Maya replied with a static tone

"Are you going to Jacob and Rose's party this weekend?" I questioned knowing the answer for sure.

"Yeah and Nick and I are helping them preparing for it. What about you?" she happily informed me

"I am coming too." I informed back and Maya stayed silent for two or three moments after that

"You have no hidden motives, right? You are not going to flirt with Rose and cause problems between her and Jacob right?" she asked in a hush with a blaming tone

"I don't." I promised and found myself caring about her opinion more than my plan, what is wrong with me?

"I hope so." she replied while doubt filled her tone but who could blame her

"May I am sorry for using you..." I repeated my apologies again hoping that she will forgive me

"It is okay." she answered back

"Can we go out for breakfast or lunch?" I asked her and the idea of seeing her made me smile

"I can't. Nick already planned our day off. Maybe next time?" She replied and I found myself seeing red again

"Are you together?" the words skipped my mouth before I can think of them

"No Nick and I are not together ." she simply replied but the man who is sitting next to her kept on yelling "Maybe soon, you will never know."

"Call me when you have some free time and I will see you at the party." I said and ended the call as she said bye.

For the rest of the day, I felt sick. I had no temperature whatsoever. I had no organ paining me more than others it was just an overwhelming pain and a feeling of sickness. I felt tired and had no will to go to the company. This is clearly a first, I never paid a girl so much attention. Attention so intense that it tortured me. I felt my heart ripping but the question that kept on replaying and echoing in my mind was : for which girl am I being this gloomy and sick? Am I suffering because of my first old love "Rose" or for the girl that I never noticed... the girl that is flipping my world around "Maya"?

Vote & comment & thank for your reads and support

What will happen next? Maya and Nick do you ship them?

Have you seen her?

Maya's Pov:

I kept on running in circles. Nothing seemed to be perfect. Nothing looked okay on me. I didn't know why but dressing up for parties always took a toll on me. Since I was kid, I had certain insecurities about my weight. I feared looking like a giant balloon when I wore colors so I always tended to dress in black, blue or grey. I tried to hid my body under baggy clothes. I did all I can to be unnoticed. I did all to be unseen.

"Yaya, wear that red dress and let us go...We are late and they are going to kill us!" Nick yelled at me and made me once again study the red dress that laid on my bed. I bought it under Nick's command. He thought that it looked "cutely sexy " his words not mine. I sighed deeply as I heard him announcing for the billionth time that we are late. I guess that I have no other choice at all.

"Good?" I questioned as I went out of my room and that's when Nick's green ocean eyes connected with mine then traveled down my body study-ing every detail about it.

"Perfect! He will certainly regret using you." He replied as he stood from the couch with a smile

"I don't actually care about him anymore. He is hers forever." I replied with a deep sigh and a broken heart

"You care and he cares. He is just too stupid to figure it out. I have a plan..." Nick's smirk turned evil and I feared what was coming next

"I don't want him and that is final. I need no plans whatsoever!" I tried to speak as confidently as possible hoping that Nick won't notice my lie.

"Remember when I came here to apologize? and how so suddenly our game of twenty questioned took a dramatic turn and you started crying about being used and rejected? " he tried to argue as he opened the door and ushered me out of my house.

"Well that made us become friends. I thought that I will never trust you again but you have been there for me since then and we became best friends. But I never said that you can trick Ian into liking me. What happened between me and him was a stupid mistake of kiss. He was driven by anger and confusion and I was too stupid to push him away!" I stubbornly tried to convince Nick that Ian means nothing too me but those stupid old tingles rushed through me as I thought of that damned stolen kiss

"What about the electrifying feelings? the sparks? You said that you felt them." Nick said with the same stubbornness

"Look I was stupid and Ian is a good looking guy. I felt nothing." I lied again and images of that stupid Greek god colonized my mind again

"Both of you are stupid but with my help...." Nick was trying to convince me again but I was too tired of his nonsense

"I swear that if you do anything wrong I will never talk to you again." I shot him a serious glare and after a minute he just nodded my way

"You know that I was just trying to care for you." Nick mumbled after a long silent ride

"I know and I appreciate it but Ian and I will never work. He will always be hers." I ended my sentence opened Nick's car door and walked to Rose and Jacob's house.

After few knocks, Rose opened the door and started blaming me for coming late. Then, she just grabbed Nick's hand and mine and dragged us in. She stopped at the threshold of the living room where now different people met and talked. I froze and took in the image in front of me looking for familiar faces. Some of our common friends were present and that made me relax more.

"You two can join anyone you want. I need to find Jacob so we can start this party properly now since you came. And Ian is here with one of his barbies." Rose spoke easily but her tone became rough and low at the end

"Thanks and sure." Nick replied to her and that's when I felt Rose's questioning glare on me.

"What?" I questioned her myself

"You seemed lost. Are you okay?" She sounded like her caring self again and I just nodded and hugged her

"You look cute by the way." She said as she hugged me and I repeated the same compliment. Rose was dress in a tight short white dress that hugged her body perfectly. She looked like a barbie herself but she had a halo of charm around her. Rose was smart and nothing like the girls that Ian usually takes interest in. She was his challenge and he will always be in love with her.

"Come on Yaya! let's meet some people and have some fun." Nick basically yelled as a child and dragged me towards the crowd

People, groups and couples, we talked to all of them. I was getting tired but nick didn't notice. He is truly a social butterfly and he enjoyed all the attention that the girls offered him. Nick can be a real gentleman at times and a real player at others.

I didn't bump into Ian for a whole hour. I guess that he either ran away to have some privacy with his date or he is being a heart broken stalker and following Rose's steps everywhere...

"May..." his husky voice echoed in my mind and tingles erupted down my spine at how real and close he sounded. I shook my head try to hold a grip on my imagination and slapped myself mentally because I need to forget him. I need to let Ian go.

"May!" he sounded more urgent and then warm fingers were placed on my bare shoulder! Damned dress, damned tingles, warmth and Ian...As I span around I saw him there right in front of me. My eyes immediately connected with his and there was that stupid homey feeling again. I felt like I belonged in his arms but I guess that he wanted nothing to do with me...Why would he?

In seconds, I looked away afraid of revealing any broken emotions. Yet even after doing so I still felt his eyes studying every inch of me. It became like a silent ritual between us; eyes, then checkup. Not a word was spoken by him and I was starting to feel uncomfortable under his gaze. Was he criticizing my style? Do I look like a balloon ? Don't I look good?

"Yaya?" Nick questioned as he cleared his throat

"Nick this Ian and Ian this is Nick." The words flew out of my mouth with me being able to lift my eyes of the floor. I heard them exchange greetings, yet Ian's tone was some how hostile? Is he still hating on Nick because of my first not so friendly date?

"May, how are you?" Ian questioned with apparent care but is he faking it because he regrets using me and kissing me or because he thinks that we are real friends?

"I am fine what about you?" I questioned and my eyes as if having a mind of their own looked up to connect with his warm chocolate brown eyes.

"Okay, I guess. How is work?" He sounded eager to know but then again why?

"It is great. We just sealed an important deal." I replied remembering the efforts that went into such a deal.

"You should see her work. She is amazing!" Nick cheered as he side hugged me

"I offered her a job but..." a flash of an unknown feeling flashed in Ian's eyes and it made me shiver

"I am sorry again Ian but I learnt everything through Nick's father and his company so I couldn't leave them when they needed me most." I felt obliged somehow to convince him that I refused his offer not because I am mad at him but because my loyalty was somewhere else.

"Now that we are best friends, you will never leave right?" Nick questioned and I saw hurt flashing in Ian's eyes but he rapidly masked it behind his cool faced so I just nodded and ignored Ian.

"Best of luck for both of you. I came over to ask about Rose. Have you seen her?" Ian asked and I froze...why does he need her? Is he still trying to make her fall for him?

"With Jacob probably ." Nick offered while his hand tightened around me for support.

"Thanks." Ian replied then offered me this weak smile as his eyes yet again studied my features one last time before he left. Before he went to search for his long lost love Rose.

"I am sorry Maya." Nick said as he hugged and I couldn't help but let some tears escape. Why did I so suddenly fell in love with my best friend's ex lover? Why did my heart race for the guy that will never notice it? He left his barbie to go find Rose and used you yet again to just know her location.......Stupid heart and Stupid Ian.

Vote & comment & thank for your reads and support

What will happen next? Maya and Nick do you ship them?

So that's Maya?

Ian's Pov

My heart finally went insane as the old and new memories flooded in my head. My heart kept on telling me to go find Rose, the woman it adored since we were kids. But my body and something way stronger than my heart kept on pulling me to Maya. I don't get why I kept on watching her from a far. I don't understand why I got a bit tensed when Nickolas wrapped her in his hands. I don't know why I stopped looking for Rose and just stared at the couple who stood hugging in the middle of the living room.

They seemed way too friendly around each other and I was left to question the nature of their relationship: are they mere friends or more? and if they are more then why do I care? I am just doing it out of a friendly care or out of something more intense? Why do I suddenly want to shove nick away and hold Maya between my own arms? What is the nature of this feeling that keeps on pulling me to her?

"Ian." Rose's voice ringed in my ear and I turned around to see her and Jacob

"Yes?" I questioned her sudden acknowledgment

"You seem lost and spacing out. Are you okay? and also your date is looking for you." she uttered with no kind of apparent emotions as if she didn't care about me bringing girls to her household.

"I am okay and she will find me..." I replied and my eyes yet again drifted to Maya again. That's when some foreign anger controlled me. Nick was hugging her close very close. He was whispering things to her and she suddenly looked at him adoringly. She, lastly, grinned at him and he kissed her forehead ever so lightly that's when my hands turned into fists and I felt my own pulse quickening. What is wrong with me?

"Are you still mad about her refusal?" Rose's voice yet again interfered with my thoughts and anger

"No but I don't trust him." I said shortly trying to keep my anger at bay

"Well he proved himself to her and us. He is still trying his best to impress her and I think that it is working..." Rose smiled as she looked at the couple

"He is scoring high on her type of guy list." Jacob talked and I don't know if his presence or his words made me more anxious and angrier

"I don't trust him." I repeated again with more venom and saw the look of surprise that took over Rose's face

"You are not asked too." Rose replied with shooting me a dirty glare

"Let's go and join them." Jacob offered Rose as he dragged her away.

I was left alone once again. I was now offered a scene of two perfect happy couples. A couple that I wanted to end and a couple that was ending my sanity. As I watched them more, I felt slender hands circle my waist and from the powerful smell of perfume I knew who it was.

"Baby...Can't we leave I am bored." My latest one night stand and now my date purred in my ear seductively.

I took a hold of her hands and moved them away from my waist. She was annoying. I woke up in my bed ,today, and she was next to me. I guess that had another drunken night. I brought here because I wanted to make Rose jealous and I also didn't want to look like a loner.

"I can't but you may leave." I harshly replied

"Who are those?" she ignored me and questioned pointing to the two couples

"You already met the hosts of this party Rose and Jacob and those are their best friends Maya and Nicholas." I clarified

"So that's Maya?" she abruptly replied after a long silence and took me by surprise how does she know her?

"You know her?" I asked rushing

"You kept on moaning her name last night." the girl clarified with no emotions apparent in her tone

"I didn't" I was now clearly shocked. I knew that sometimes I moaned Rose's name before but I never did that to any other girl!

"Well you were way too drunk to remember." my date answered me then walked away leaving with an information that weighed tones! Why would I fantasize about Maya? Do I want her in a physical way? she is not my type even...She is way too simple and pure. She is not exactly a model. She doesn't look as good as Rose....

Questions kept on haunting me for the rest of the party. I didn't know what was happening around me and just took a seat on one of the living room sofas and sat there for god knows how much. I didn't move and my head rested in my hands all that time until I felt a light tap on my shoulder and there was Maya in her red dress. I didn't notice it earlier because Nick kept on getting on my nerves. The dress reached her mid thigh and left her long legs uncovered. It hugged her every curve perfectly and showed that she was no more overweight but just perfectly curvy.

"You look beautiful." The words escaped my mouth before I could stop them and Maya's cheeks became as red as her dress

"Thanks and it all thanks to Nick's help." She shyly replied yet the mention of his name got me to lose my temper again

"Nick?" I roughly questioned her

"He picked the dress." she simply replied but I saw a look of concern in her eyes. I knew that she certainly felt my anger and was questioning it. Without giving her a chance to talk or to run away I just caught her hand and found myself driven by some kind of maddened instinct to claim her as mine. She kept on yelling at me but I released her only when we were alone in the corridor.

"Ian what the hell is wrong with you!" She yelled at me

"You are what's wrong with me!" I yelled back at her and took a step closer to her while she stepped back and hit the wall

"What did I do to you? And aren't you afraid of Rose catching us?" She hushed this time and tried to look anywhere but my eyes

"She has guests to care about." I replied as I closed the space between us and heard Maya's sharp intake of air

"Ian?" she questioned again while her eyes kept down but I myself had no answer for her. I myself didn't know what I was doing. I felt like my body was moving on its own. My hand rested under her chin and slightly and delicately pushed her head up so that our eyes connected with each other for a while. Then my eyes drifted to her plump lips and without missing another second my lips collided with hers in a passionate kiss. She struggled against me. She tried to push me but like what happened in the first kiss after few seconds she started to respond to me and I lost myself in this intoxicating kiss. I have kissed thousands of girls before but I never felt a fire igniting within me until now. Even when I kissed Rose before I never felt this way...

"Why?" Maya breathlessly asked after our need of air kicked in and forced us to stop the kiss

"I don't know..." I replied honestly then waited for a bit and rushed out of Rose's house leaving Maya in the corridor alone

Vote & comment & thank for your reads and support

What will happen next?

"I hate you."

V ote & comment & thank for your reads and support

Ian's Pov

I had to meet some of my coworkers for lunch today and as usual I picked the same restaurant "Chez Balzak". The moment I stepped foot in it. I heard this slight faraway giggle. It was as enchanting as a melody and it lured me to follow it but I knew better than that!

the first person who saluted me was the same stupid waiter from my date with Maya. I remember how his eyes traveled and studied every inch of her body. I remember how his eyes became a shade darker when he gazed at her curves. I remembered it all and found myself getting angrier by the second.

What happened after my second kiss with Maya? well I ran as fast as I can and avoided her and Rose for the past two weeks. My dreams were haunted by these two girls lately and I found no pleasure in being with other women. Once I put my head to rest on my pillow, I will start thinking about Rose and how I should get her. But, once my eyes become heavy, all I could see was Maya, her curves, lips and giggle.

"This is going to be awkward." Bryan supposedly mumbled as he showed me my table but I heard him. What the hell is that suppose to mean?

The same hypnotizing laugh ringed again and echoed. This time it wasn't as faint. It was clear and tempting. It was full of hope and life not like the now empty restaurant. It was still early for lunch but one of my coworkers begged us to start early because he has some family obligations to attend to.

Again with that laugh, I tried to stop myself from turning and searching for its source. I wanted to focus now on my present coworkers who were discussing a very important matter but when the laugh continued to echo the restaurant every ten minutes, I just gave up and turned around. Yet I was never expecting such shock.

There was the same girl I kissed two weeks ago. There she was on a table right behind me. How didn't I notice her before? Well maybe because rage blinded me when I remembered how Bryan flirted with her in front of me? Maya sat there with a man in front of her. He was not Nick. This guy was blond and his eyes were clearly fixed on Maya. The latter seemed happy and that flipped my mood in seconds.

She was wearing this body hugging white dress. It looked good on her and displayed every curve she had. Her usually naturally straight black hair had new waves and volume to it and I felt my hand itching wanting to run through it and see how soft it is. She still had the very minimum of makeup but her cheeks looked red. She was blushing to this guy! God knows what he have been telling her!

Something inside me ticked and I for a reason wanted to go yell at her. But what rights do I have when it comes to her? I am nothing to her and she should be my noting. I shouldn't think of her but all I could see now was flashes of both kisses, how her lips felt against mine, how sweet she tasted, how hesitant she was at first and then how she relaxed and made me get lost in those kisses.

"Ian? are you okay?" My colleague asked me and that got me out of my trance

"Do you know her?" another asked and I stiffened should I lie to my friends or tell them that that girl was confusing me and making my world spin

"Yes..." I replied as I gazed at her and found her date reaching for her hand. When he captured it and she didn't drew it away my blood started boiling and my gaze was set on their hands.

"Are you jealous?" another asked and I just shook my head. Why would I be jealous if she means nothing to me?

I tried my best to ignore her and her giggles. If she is happy, I should be happy for her too. She suddenly stood up with her date and went out. A sound in my head echoed with a command and every fibber in my being wanted to do it, to follow her and stop whatever was going to happen next on their date....A kiss, a make out, maybe even more....

"Go after her if you want. We are already leaving." one of my friends offered and I nodded.

I don't know why but I felt protective of her. I mean she can date but the least she can do is to introduce the guy first to us, her friends. Does she consider me as a friend? Or does she hate me for stealing two kisses and planing to use her?

those questions melted away as I saw her date facing her and then closing the space that was left between them.My heart raced at such a sight and I took few steps walking their way rapidly. What the hell am I doing? I questioned myself but didn't care much. I need to stop this because it was causing me a pang of pain...Maybe just maybe I want to sleep with Maya, just like any other girl, a one nightstand to get her once and for all out of my system.

Before, I reached them the guy looked lovingly at her and she returned the feels. My hands as always turned into fists and I stopped dead in track as the man leaned in and Kissed her forehead.

"Maya!" I angrily shouted as the man left her to get into her car. She just froze for a minute and then looked at me with wide eyes.

"Ian?" she questioned and my heart raced when she uttered my name

"What were you doing! are you cheating on Nick?" I asked as I stepped closer to her and she as always backed away to be met with her car.

"I was on a date." she clarified and I saw red

"Didn't you hate this place before? So why were your fake laughs echoing in it" I pointed how hypocritical she sounded

"I do hate it but he picked the place..." She answered in a small voice

"So no more Miss pure but a hypocritical cheating WHO..." I was seething with anger for a reason and I didn't think about what I was saying.

"Don't you dare! How low do you think of me? Nick is my friend. He actually sat this date up." she yelled and now her face was red of anger and I think tears were forming in here dark orbs

"And should believe that?" I yelled at her again

"Why do you even care! Just go and swoon some girl or Rose! Just let me be." she yelled back with the same fire and anger and tried to turn her back to me so she can climb in her car seat and run away.

But I found myself hating that idea and once again the need to claim her as mine took over my brain and all my senses. So I just grabbed her hand, turned her back to face me and connected my lips with hers. As always she tried to fight me off but that only ignited a fire in me and in minutes that fire burned both our souls as we talked our anger through our lips and tongues. My hands intertwined in her silky hair and then slowly started to move and appreciate every curve of her body. This kiss was more passionate and heated and when I had to set her lips free so she can breath, I found myself kissing her neck. She gasped and tried to push me but I pinned her hands and continued till I found her sweet spot and sucked on it. I kissed her and enjoyed every reaction of hers, every shiver, every moan but when she mumbled my name I had to stop or else this was take another intimate level...

"Why?" she breathlessly questioned and I couldn't but gaze at her. I wanted to memorize every little detail about her. I wanted Maya and that was final. But how could I when I love Rose and Just Rose?

"I don't know..." I repeated the same damned answer but as I looked at her new hickey I knew exactly what I did and why I did it. I marked her so that guy can back off.

"I hate you." She yelled at me and hurried to her car leaving me to flinch at the echo of her words. She hates me but why should I care when I love another? I should just go see Rose and forget about Maya.

Vote & comment & thank for your reads and support

What will happen next?

Facing Ian

Hello everyone and sorry for the belated chapter but here you guys go

Maya's pov

That stupid man had to give me a hickey! I hate him! I hate his passionate tantrums! I loath how he finds it okay to kiss me whenever he pleases! I hate Ian. The last time I saw him I was on a date, a blind date sat by Nick. Nick vowed to me that Asher is the perfect guy for me. I wanted to prove him wrong but the date was perfect. Asher was a gentleman and accepted all my terms. He was funny and charming. He is a pediatrician and he has the kindest heart ever. I enjoyed everything about our date but I never expected how it ended. That stupid idiot, Ian, had to ruin it for me.

"Ian was definitely jealous" Nick announced as I told him what happened yesterday

"Ian is just looking for a plan B to make Rose jealous." I repeated again and again. Ian cannot get jealous over me. He feels nothing towards me. I am basically his nothing and that is why I need to get rid of any romantic feelings I have about him. I need to focus on anything and anyone but Ian.

"He is just cornering you and forcing himself on you when no one is around to make Rose jealous?" Nick repeated in a sarcastic tone

"He knows that I will tell her..." I tried to argue pointlessly

"He is not stupid. He knows that your friendship is way more important to you. He knows that for the sake of Rose you will keep your feelings and the kisses a mere secret." Nick declared while continuing to rest on my sofa

"It is late aren't you going home?" I questioned trying to change the subject because Nick did really figure me out.

I am keeping everything hidden from Rose. And I will always keep my growing feelings for Ian at bay. I will ignore how he makes me feel when his skin connects with mine or when his lips are dancing over mine. Rose is more important to me...Ian is hopefully just a fling. He is temporary just like his hickey.

"So you do have feelings for him? Should I tell Asher to forget about you?" Nick teased more

"You have to leave now and don't tell Asher a thing..." I playfully yet seriously warned him because I need to move on

"Okay, okay , I will leave but you will see me first thing tomorrow morning. We have a conference with Mr. Ian himself..." Nick said as he stood up

"I wasn't informed..." I shockingly replied

"I guess that he found it awkward to call you so he directly contacted me." Nick explained

"I am not coming tomorrow!" I rushed yelling

"You are coming and this time you will not allow him to use you. Tell him that you are already taken." Nick informed me as he started to walk away toward the door

"But I am not..." I replied honestly because Asher and I didn't plan a second date till now but Ash was texting me all the time since our date

"Asher said that he will be asking you for a second date." Nick smilingly said and waved goodbye but why did the latter information didn't make me happy?

At night, all the kisses I shared with Ian replayed in my head in slow motion. All his features got painted in my mind and my heart started humming. My fingers traveled to the hickey that he left on my neck and that's when tears filled my eyes. I am falling for a player. I love an already taken guy.

I cried my heart out that night. I have never been this hopeless. I feel like I am losing all control over my life. I have never been this emotional at least not since high school and all the bullying about my weight .

I cried all night as memories invaded my mind. I felt weak but I knew that I had to act strong. I am going to face Ian soon, in matter of few hours. So when dawn came , I decided to build my walls up and be the fighter that I once was.

"Since your company is still new, can you tell us in what way will merging it with ours, will do us good?" Nick asked Ian as the conference started

"My company may be new but the profits that it is making are higher than some older companies. Our services are amazing and my team is very punctual and hard working. We will offer you profit, assured success , and a loyal hard working team." Ian replied with confidence yet at his last words he throw the dirtiest look at me...Does he still believe that I am cheating on Nick? Is he this insane?

"My team is very loyal and I doubt that any team can be better than them but we will see." Nick responded decoding the dirty message behind Ian's glare.

The conference continued for two long hours. The longest hours of my life Ian kept on throwing me the nastiest glare of all. But what he did at the end of the conference was the straw that broke the camel's back. He looked at Nick and me then waited till all people left and uttered the sentence that stabbed me like a dagger.

"if you are searching for loyal people, I need to advice you to reconsider some of your teammates." He told nick while looking at me angrily.

"Watch it...." Nick tried to defend me but I stopped him with my hand and ordered him to leave.

After being left alone with Ian, I stood and faced him. We were standing on different sides of the table but both of us stayed rooted in our places.

"Mr. Mathews." I angrily spat and saw Ian's taken aback features " Listen closely because I am going to say this once only. You and I are not friends. You don't know me and you have no right to interfere in my life. Yes you think that we are friends but I just discovered how low you think of me. I will not be treated like trash or like a nothing. You have no right to kiss me and then disappear. You have no right to even talk to me. So starting this moment I will only respond of the topic is either work related or Rose related other than that we go our separate ways. Lastly to clarify things in your dirty mind, I would like to tell you that I will never be a cheater. I am actually getting into a serious relationship...Now if you excuse me I would like you to stay out of my life forever." I yelled at him letting all my anger out.

"May...." Ian uttered in indescribable tone

"Miss Mayer to you and I will tell Nick to accept your proposal because it is honestly promising but as I said before you may not address me unless the topic is work related. Now goodbye." I repeated and stormed out leaving Ian behind. I will build my walls up so high that he or any other guy won't hurt me again.

Pregnant and Stay

I an's Pov

Can a person hate his own freaking last name?

Well thanks to Maya, now , I do hate or even loath mine.

"Mr. Mathews" that was all she used to acknowledge me since my company merged with Nickolas's, one week ago.

I thought that by merging the companies and moving to a new office in Nickolas's company was going to be beneficial and that somehow I will be able to ask for Maya's forgiveness but the latter didn't cross my way. I didn't see her around , well at least not alone. She was always with Nick and even if I intruded and interfered in their friendly conversations, her only acknowledgements of me were my last name and some nodding.

She said that we are not friends. That statement may sound truthful to her and to others but it kind of caused me a great pain. I don't know why but I felt a kind of a pull for Maya. I never really knew her as a person but since that doomed wedding day, her name brought a smile to my face and her picture constantly popped in my dreams and thoughts.

I tried to find reasons to why I started to angrily kiss her whenever I saw her with another guy, I tried to explain why I marked her neck with a hickey, I tried to do my best to question my obsessive need of her being near me but I found no answer.

All I know is that Maya is not my type. She not blond, skinny or has a barbie-like figure. She is just a curvy brunette with dark vibrant eyes. She was not sophisticated and classy but feisty and kind. Most of all Maya was not needy like all the girls I dated. No she was independent and in no need for me.

She said it wide and clear she has no place for me in her life. But something in me needs her.

I might be unneeded. But she is not.

For the very first time I am being the rejected instead of the reject(er) and let me tell you that this position is hellish.

I got frustrated again and tried to get Maya out of my head. I looked at the file between my hands but my brain kept on repeating the same questions " why am I chasing Maya?" "Do I want her as a friend or more? and is this more emotional or mere physical?" "How could I care about a girl this much when I am already in love with another?" " Why did I suddenly stopped thinking about Rose? My Rose. My perfect woman. The one I loved since I was a teen. The one that I promised to win her love again and start a family with her...

I am in love with Rose but Maya became a distraction instead of a means to get to Rose!

I need to stay away from Maya and focus on Rose, my Rose.

As I made my goals clear again a faint giggle reached my ears. It was faint yet I felt like it was mocking my plans. I knew who it belonged to. I knew it because it tormented me before and it still does. I diverted my eyes from the file between my hands and looked at the glass wall that separated my office from the rest of the company and there she was "Maya". She was standing with Nick and another guy waiting for the elevator. The latter looked familiar. I think that he is the same guy from her restaurant date. In moments that guy's hand sneaked behind Maya and enveloped her in a tight side hug. I continued to watch waiting for a violent reaction from her but nothing...Instead, she in few seconds leaned her head on his shoulder and hugged his waist...

The scene continued to play in front of me for god knows how much time and then the elevator dinged announcing that it reached the floor. Will she leave with him? My breathes suddenly hitched and my heart crazily throbbed against my chest. I felt some pain starting in the pit of my stomach and then reaching my chest...What the hell is wrong with me?

I wanted to look away...I wanted but my eyes were glued on that curvy stubborn girl...I watched how she looked at that guy...How his eyes traveled from her eyes to her lips then back to her lips. I saw her blushing and looking down. Then a proud happy smile appeared on the man's face and in slow motion he leaned down to her and captured her lips in a slow kiss.

I looked away back to the file in my hands and somehow I found on two pieces.

Dammit why did I feel a sudden void in my chest? Why do I feel nothing?

For the rest of the day, I tried to work. Tried is a keyword because I didn't do much.

I didn't do much and I didn't even go out of my office, not for lunch, not for even a glass of water...

"Group dinner tonight, hope that you will come." I read the text that Rose sent to me but surprisingly found no will in me to attend.

but this might be a sign and a chance to get Rose, I argued with myself and sent her a text asking about the time and place.

In two hours, we all , and by all I mean Maya her date who is named Asher, Nick and Rose and Jack, were sitting in Rose's house. The latter was dressed amazingly and when she opened the door I couldn't help but admire her beauty. She was truly a real life barbie doll. I kept on flirting with her when her husband wasn't around and she seemed way too happy to mind my hidden messages. I was the first comer to her house and because of that I had more than half an hour of alone time with Rose. Her husband didn't mind me and just left us in the living room. What an idiot!

I kept on talking with Rose endlessly but whenever she laughed I couldn't help but remember a certain giggle. What the hell is wrong with me?

Talking to Rose and being with her alone seemed so familiar. It made me smile and be comfortable. Dear god how much I have missed her. I just wanted to hug her?...yet why not kiss her roughly and possessively the way I acted around Maya ?

"Maya." Rose yelled as we heard the doorbell and as she expected it was really Maya ,her date and Nick.

"Rose" the girls embraced happily but when my eyes found Maya's eyes her happy orbs turned emotionless.

"Hey guys..." I saluted as I stood and walked to them stretching my arm

"hey man." Nick said as he shook my hand then it was May's turn

"Mr. Mathews." she responded and reluctantly offered me her smaller hand. My hand held hers and then I felt an overwhelming kind of warmth. I didn't want to let go of her hand but the man next to her cleared his throat as if asking me to back off.

"This is my date Asher." Maya spoke and smiled lovingly at the man at her right and at that moment felt sick

"Nice to meet you" I lied through clutched teeth

"Nice to meet you too." he replied and since that moment side hugged Maya till it was dinner time.

"WE have an announcement." Rose said as she smiled at her husband and I as usual hated their connection " MayMay, you have to open this small box and then you will know." Rose happily sang as she offered Maya a small box. The latter did as told and opened it to find a bracelet with something curved on it...

"Aunty..." she read in a small voice then a tear fell down her cheek then in a rush she stood and ran to hug Rose...

Pregnant! My Rose is pregnant! For the second time today I felt some kind of pain taking over my body.

After dinner, spacing out and some fake acting, I managed to leave early. I drove aimlessly. I felt like a loser and a loner. The girl who is supposed to be my friend just threw me out of her life and the girl who is the love of my life is pregnant with another man's baby...What a life. I drove in empty roads for god knows how much time then headed to a bar...alcohol might help me forget...

Maya's Pov:

Some noise was trying to pull me out of my dream land. I tried my best to ignore it but it kept on repeating itself...What the hell is it...As I woke up I discovered that it was my stupid doorbell but who could be here at such a late hour?... It is only four am !

I went to the door and heard some muffled voice calling my name and because of that I relaxed and opened the door. But to say that I was surprised right now would be an understatement. There he was leaning his weight on my door frame but he didn't look as powerful as usual. He looked lost and broken...

"May..." he said and then trough all his weight on me as he hugged me

"Mr. Mathews, what are you doing here?" I asked as I tried my best to keep on standing and not crushing to the ground with him

"She is pregnant..." he brokenly uttered and then hugged me more tightly. I froze. don't know why but I just stood motionless. Is it because he hugged me? or because he came for me seeking comfort or because he is crying over Rose and yet again using me...?

"She is no more My Rose..." he said then sniffed and I felt his tears fall on my shoulder and neck where he rested his head.

"Mr. Mathews...let's go inside..." I offered and helped him all the way to my couch. Yet his next action took me again by surprise he sat next to me and then I felt his head being placed in my lap. He looked like a tired kid and I couldn't stop my fingers from touching his smooth hair.

"Mr.Mathews..." I uttered in a few trying to get his attention. I just wanted to know why did he come here? Yet suddenly he turned around now with his face facing my stomach, he snuggled as close as possible.

"I hate it when you call me that." he sounded like a kid and i found it ...cute?

"Mr. Mathews...we agreed to no longer cross roads." i stubbornly informed him...I am just tired of feeling broken whenever he talks about his love for Rose.

"Ian....Ian...I..A..N" he repeatedly said against my stomach and I couldn't help but smile at how this grown man is acting.

"Mr.Mathews, you need to leave." I calmly informed him again

"I feel comfortable whenever I am around you. You feel warm and good..." Ian mumbled as he if possible get closer to me

"Mr. Mathews ?!" I questioned

"Can we just stay like this? I somehow need you ,just you, to be here for me..." he continued to talk and my heart started racing

"You need someone to help you forget Rose and I cannot allow you to use me again..." I hushed to him and at that moment he sat and faced me

"I need you...You have some powers over me...I don't know what are they but all I know is that I need you May...Please don't let me suffer alone...!" he begged and sounded as broken and tired as ever. His eyes were filled with tears and unspoken emotions and I found myself wanting to kiss his pain away...but I cannot go back to that same situation ...

"May...please!" he begged again

"Mr..." I was about to utter his last name but when I saw the sadness that overcame his orbs I felt bad "Ian" I uttered shakily for no obvious reason

"I missed that" he said a hugged me tightly

"Ian...You are suffocating me..." I hardly spoke fighting for air

"sorry, I just needed that." he murmured as he slowly let go of me

"It is okay" I hushed at him and looked down feeling my cheeks burning and kept on silently praying for the dim light miss and hide my blushing cheeks

"Stay with me tonight..." Ian demanded in a low husky tone and that when thousands of butterflies erupted in my stomach

"Ian...I..." I wanted to find some words to refuse and move away but words seemed to fail me as he kept on staring at my eyes

"Just like this..." he said and that's when his head was back to its former place and he snuggled to my stomach again

"Ian, this is not right...Asher..." I tried to make him understand to feel him only become stiff and then snuggling closer to the point of me be afraid of even breathing

"Let's forget about all just for tonight...I never felt this safe before...It is like you are my home...There is this strange pull to you and I am just going with it...Just for tonight May..." he begged and I surrendered the moment he called me home

I am his "home"? He feels "safe" with me?

"okay" I agreed and he took my hand placed in his mouth and I froze as his smooth hot lips planted a kiss on my palm

"Thank you May..." he mumbled and after that seemed to get lost in a deep sleep.

Dear god how am I going to act with such a guy? How am I going to push him away ? how am going to refuse his friendly behavior when he can be this affectionate and cute ? why is my heart beating wildly for him and not for Asher ? What am I going to do when I know that Ian is just using me to forget about Rose and her new coming baby ...

Vote & comment please

what is going to happen next ???

"Coffee, tea, juice, Friends?"

Ian's Pov

Cuddling! How I refused to do such an exaggerated act before but tables flipped around and now all I wanted is to snuggle to this warm figure next to me. I pushed my head closer to it and that's when I heard a surprised gasp of air...

"Ian...Wake up." a sweet voice invaded my ears and somehow drew a smile on my face

"Ian...Ian..." she repeated and that's when I flipped around to face my talker.

"May...Good morning." I uttered and then started to study her morning look. She looked tired but she was still smiling. I knew that I caused her tiredness because sitting for hours on a sofa is not that comfortable and I also woke her up way too early.

"Good morning." she said back offering me a smile that made my own lips turn into a smile.

She has simple features yet in a way they all looked angelic. Even if her hair was put in a messy bun and even when she had no makeup at all she looked good. My eyes found their usual way to her lips and there was that perfect smooth set of light pink lips. I remember how they felt against mine and found myself acting upon such memories...I wanted to kiss Maya...again for unknown reasons.

"Ian?" she questioned and then as if she understood my intention she placed her hand on my chest and pushed me back

"We cannot do this anymore...I am dating Asher and you and I are..." She seemed at a loss of words

"We are friends " I filled in the blank spaces in her definition of us

"Friends do not kiss each other. Friends do not use each other. Friends know each other's real persona...but we don't. We are mere strangers." she tried to argue but I saw a glimpse of pain in her eyes

"How could you allow a stranger to sleep here on you lap? how could care for a stranger the same way you cared for me...We are friends Maya. Friends with a certain emotional pull...A pull that I do not understand. ..I can't help it but want to kiss you whenever you are around" I said honestly as I sat up and faced her. She blushed hearing my words but that look of pain and hurt never erased completely.

"I felt that kind of emotional pull too but I cannot be in a friends with benefit type of relation...Asher is offering me what I want a real relation. ..but with you I will always be a hidden dirty secret...I will be your plan B after Rose...I will be always a rebound...And I cannot do that to myself... I can't act on a stupid pull...It is just temporary as soon as we kiss each other we can go weeks without seeing or contacting one another...It is just not healthy...We both can do better." Maya finished her speech and then stood from the sofa and I felt the same violent kind of pain bursting in my chest.

"Only you can have such an effect on me...I have been a player all my life and girls said hurtful things to me all the time when I broke their hearts but I never felt such pain...When you reject me I feel like my heart is going to stop beating ." I hushed looking for an explanation

"Because I am hurting your pride...You are for once rejected and not the reject(er)" Maya tried to explain as she moved and walked to her kitchen

"can you not push me anymore? I am sorry for being rude, for being a jerk and for all my nonsense...May I need you?" I begged and saw her seriously studying my features. Is she trying to discover if I am lying or not?

"Coffee, tea, juice, Friends?" Maya finally uttered and smiled brightly at me and I couldn't help but smile right back at her

"For real?" I questioned to make sure and she nodded with a hug smile plastering on her face and I couldn't help but walk to her hug her and spin her around.

"Ian let go of me or I will it take back" she yelled giggling

"Okay...okay...I am just happy..." I smiled down at her as I released her from my grip

" Now Mr.Mathews..." she tried to talk but I grumbled at her

"I mean Ian, We have few rules to go through so this friendship can last." she corrected and I nodded at her waiting to hear her rules "first no kissing. Second we cannot use each other unless we discuss what is happening. Third we will try to know the real us. Fourth if you are still trying to break Rose and Jacob then I will never be a part of your plans and sixth, we will truly look for the best for each other." She explained all the rules and I nodded even though a sound in me kept on saying that I want more

"Okay..." agreed happily at least now we are not fighting anymore "so now what do you want for breakfast? coffee, tea, juice and waffles, pancakes or crepes, eggs and bacon ?" she numerated my options

"Can't we eat outside?" I offered not willing to tire her more

"Are you doubting my skills in the kitchen Mr.Mathews?" She teased and I grumbled hearing my last name again

"Maybe Miss Mayer maybe..." I teased her back and saw a childish glow around her

"Well take a seat then and you will receive the best breakfast you will ever have in no time..." she happily sung and went to the stove and I was left to watch her sing, dance and cook

Vote & comment to get the next chapter

chocolate Fondant & backless dress

Maya's Pov:

The little smile that drew on his face as he ate his breakfast made my day. I loved challenges and him doubting my cooking abilities made me do my best...Is Ian bringing the best in me? I shook that idea out of my head and heard him moaning in acceptance as the dark chocolate melted from his chocolate fondant.

"This is the best breakfast ever..." he commented in a childish hyper tone and I couldn't help but smile at him happily

"Well thank you Mr. Mathews." I teased him as the spoon full of chocolate goodies entered his mouth and he happily sighed

"Why didn't you teach Rose how to cook and bake?" Ian questioned and I once again felt uneasy hearing him talking about Rose...He will always do...He loves her I argued in my mind

"She is not into this kind of activities." I said in a low tone and that earned me a nod from Ian

"She loves fancy food but could never cook...Once when we were younger she tried to make some desert recipe and nearly burned down the house." he joked

"She nearly burned down my house just because she tried to make popcor n..." I remembered that day and smiled at the memory of Rose apologizing for the hundredth time

"But we have to admit that she has a brilliant personality and she is an amazing fashionista, a classy and a sophisticated women and a beautiful breathtaking girl..." Ian uttered describing Rose with this faraway look on his face...he looked like a tortured lover willing to do anything to have his princess by his side...

"She amazing." I agreed and started to play around with my food. My appetite now seemed to be gone ...

"Does she love him ?" Ian asked after few quite moments and I wanted to yell at him to change the subject because heaven knows why but his every word about Rose tortured me

"She learned to and she is having his baby so that may answer your ques tion..." I replied kind of rudely and stood up taking my plate in hand and left Ian alone

"Are you okay?" he murmured as he followed me to the kitchen and I tried to play it cool as much as possible

"Yeah, I am by the way what time is it?" I questioned as Ian got closer to me and for a reason stopped just an inch away...What the hell is he doing? Is he going to break my first rule? Is he going to kiss me after talking emotionally about my best friend ? Questioned stormed in my head and I found myself eager for that stupid not so real kiss...

"It is eleven thirty..." Ian replied in a husky voice or was my imagination playing tricks on me!

"eleven thirty...eleven thirty..."I repeated feeling like I forgot something then it hit me I am going on a date with Asher in an hour ...Remembering Ash, I took steps back away from Ian then ran to my room leaving the latter totally surprised

"what is wrong May?" Ian yelled questioning as he banged on my room door

"I have a date with Ash in an hour." I yelled back as I started going through my dresses and outfits "and I need to take a shower,do my hair and makeup and dress up" I continued but there was no respond just total silence

Ian's Pov:

Date...

Ash...

those two words froze me and I felt my self getting alarmed, then frustrated, then angry and as usual possessive and protective...Is this a friendly reaction? can this be normal in our sort of relation? I stood there looking at her door with my hands still as fists and I didn't know what I should do...

When she stood and ran, I thought that my talk about Rose angered her...I feared her thinking that I am yet again using her but then a slight sly thought played in my mind...Can she be jealous? but why would she when we are just friends and why would I want her to be jealous?

There was chocolate on the corner of her mouth, I spotted it as soon as I walked to her kitchen and to it my body react instantly. I walked closer to her and saw her freeze...Every time we were at such proximity I end up kissing her and savoring the taste those lips of hers ...I wanted to do just do but then she asked about time and well ran off

I walked back to the same sofa that we spent the previous night on and sat there quietly watching TV ...I gave up my staring contest with the door as it was of no use and May wouldn't come out. She is dressing up and dolling up for another man while I am feeling like shit! I should really take a hold of my life and maybe start dating for once...

"Ian?" Maya questioned as she walked to me and I swear that I saw a halo surrounding her. She was dressed in a hot pink dress that hugged and showed all her curves, her lips were covered in this very smooth layer of pink lip gloss, and then her luscious black hair was let loose in a wavy way. My heart beat quickened as I saw her and then she turned around giving me a full view of her backless dress...smooth skin that's all I saw but then I imagined her date putting his hand on the small of her back and a grumble escaped my lips

"You don't like it ?" Maya questioned and a pained hurt kind of look mirrored in her eyes and I didn't know how I am supposed to answer her because I didn't know why I was feeling suddenly protective of her

"It is not like that but a backless dress might give your date the wrong ideas" I tried to clear things out without giving any emotional insight on how hot and bothered she is making me

"Oh...Ash is not like that...He is a gentleman and I this is our third date... He knows me pretty well ..." she explained and for a reason her eyes would not leave the floor

"but some people think that the third date is the charm..." I argued more wishing for her to just get that dress off and wear a turtleneck or even stay home and cancel the date

"I told him that I am ..." She mumbled slowly and I swear that all her skin became pinkish while her cheeks became as red as a tomato

"You are what?" I urged her to continue her statement and she took a deep breath

"You cannot laugh, promise me" she begged and I nodded kind of anticipating what's next "I am a virgin and I am not ready...Not until I make sure that I found the one" She announced and I felt some wired sense of happiness...What the hell is wrong with me. i usually do not do virgins! they just cause drama and expect way too much emotional crap

"You think he could be the one?" I asked after clearing my throat

"He is a very nice guy; he appreciates my opinions, shares a lot of my common interests and cares about me...I don't love him but I can see my self growing to do so" Maya informed me and I just nodded as we heard the door knock and she ran to it like a kid running to sit on santa's lap ...too excitedly and happily !

Waiting for your comments to update what do u think should happen next ?

Earlier was awkward

- -

Ian's Pov :

the situation now cannot be described in any term other than awkward.

After Maya and that freaking dude Asher left, I stayed behind in Maya's house. I didn't know if I should leave or stay...Wait or go find a one nig htstand...I was lost...until I heard a knock and that's when I thought that Maya is back. I ran to the door like a kid. I thought that she canceled her date but as I opened the door, shock took over me...There stood the one and only ...Rose.

"Ian...What the hell are you doing here and where is Maya?...Maya" she yelled with a tensed look

Rose looked the same as always. She is always dressed perfectly. Every outfit of hers showed a high taste and an appreciation for fashion. Her golden hair swayed in the air and shinned like a halo illuminating her. Her blue orbs...the ones that I adore looked like a storming...

"Maya..." Rose yelled more and I stopped eyeing her

"She is not home." I informed her

"Well what the hell are you doing here ?" Rose said furiously and pushed me aside to get in

"Maya and I are friends and friends visit each other like you are doing now..." I fired at her and for once I felt annoyed with Rose's possessiveness and control over Maya

"You were never her friend...In fact, you never gave her a second look before." Rose yelled back at me

"Well I was an idiot back then. " I tried to defend myself but right now I knew for sure that I was an idiot

"Maybe because she was a little overweight but now that she lost some pounds you want to get her in your bed" Rose accused me as she sat on the living room couch and I couldn't deny that the idea of sleeping with Maya had crossed my mind endlessly...but could Rose be jealous?

"What if I want to bed her?" I shot at Rose as I stood next to her way too close if I may add

"I won't let you" she yelled and challenged me looking me right in the eyes.

She didn't expect our faces to be that close and I didn't expect her to freeze but she did. We both continued to study each other's faces and I found this usual comfort in Rose's eyes but for a reason my eyes didn't drift downward...My gaze never reached her lips...Not like it does with Maya...There was no pull...No intensity! Maybe my heart finally accepted that it has to let go ?

"Guys?" I heard the questioning statement and it brought me out of my head in no time...there was Maya looking shocked, hurt, in pain?

"Maya" Rose and I yelled at the same time and jumped away from each other

"MayMay..." Rose uttered coolly as she walked to Maya and hugged her but the latter's eyes we set on me and in them was this new kind of void

"Rose, what are you doing here?" Maya questioned in a small voice and I knew immediatly that she would rather be anywhere but here

"I came to check on you but I was surprised to find Ian here ..." Rose admitted

"I am surprised too he should have left like half an hour ago..." Maya explained kind of sharply and threw me a silent glare

"I didn't know what to do when you left for your date..." I slowly explained but got only a nod as an answer

"So why are back so rapidly when you only left half an hour ago?" Rose asked with fear and care

"I forgot my phone..." Maya answered as she pointed to her living room table and there was her phone

"Asher is here ?" Rose continued to ask

"Yeah in the car he is waiting for me " Maya nodded as she answered

"Can I meet him?" Rose asked in a childish hyper way

"Sure...Why not I guess..." Maya answered after a moment and walked to the door leading the way...

"May..." Asher saluted her with a hug again and I tensed and froze

"Ash...I was gone for like ten minutes!" she smiled at him sweetly and a low grumble roared in my chest

"Long enough for me to miss you..." he replied with a grin and continued to act like a teen in love

"Silly" Maya teased him then turned to us " These are my friends Rose and Ian." she introduced us in very formal way

"Nice to meet you both." Asher politely saluted us

"So Asher how did you get to know our Maya..." Rose asked and I found myself wanting to know all the details about their stupid relation

"Well Nick is my friend and lately he kept talking about this girl " a fireball" he called her and I got intrigued. I heard him describing her ...beautiful, hyper, independent, strong, forgiving, kind... then he finally showed me her picture and then I kind of wanted to know her in person so Nick set us up." Asher explained and side hugged Maya closely next to him and the latter blushed. Her cheeks turned deep red and her dark orbs shinned adoringly as they studied Asher. Then all I saw is red. I wanted to rip her out of his grip and hold her tight in my hands. I wanted to punch that guy once, twice or a million time....Outraged that's how I felt

"That's so sweet but if you ever hurt her I will find you and break your neck " Rose threatened and Asher looked at her amusingly then nodded and promised to cherish Maya

"Earlier was awkward. I hope that Maya ddn't get the wrong ideas. I have to explain the situation to her ..." Rose breathed heavily as we walked away from the couple allowing them to go back to their freaking date

"It was..." I simply replied because images of Maya and Asher making out on their date kept torturing me

"Are you okay?" Rose asked as her hand shot and held mine and suddenly I realized it there were no sparks anymore

"Yeah" I replied faintly as I withdrew my hand

"You are falling for her." Rose's shocked announcement stopped my tracks and I froze how can I e in love with a simple girl? a girl other than Rose? an already taken girl?

Again WAITING FOR YOUR COMMENTS TO UPDATE

WHAT WILL ROSE'S REACTION BE ? How will Ian deal with his new emotions? and Did Maya get the wrong ideas ?

Angry is an understatement

Numb, that's how I felt after seeing their near kiss. Their faces were so close. Lips one inch apart. Eyes gazing lovingly at each other. The same air being breathed by both and probably the same heartbeat pace. Yesterday as I walked in to get my phone, I went through a storm of emotions, loss, defeat, sadness, sorrow and then anger but I hid it well. I masked it all and acted cool but till now I feel broken, damaged, numb.

"So?" the same manly voice that colonized my dreams said interrupting my session of woe.

"So?" I repeated kind of harshly as I turned to see him entering the company's staff room

"What's up?" Ian continued to ask as he walked closer to me

"Nothing is up." I fired at him and turned back to the coffee machine

Silence invaded the room after so. Only the drops of coffee made a sound. It was definitely awkward. I wanted earth to open up and swallow me. I wished for Ian to leave but the smell of his perfume assured me that he is still here and close by. As got absorbed into my own ideas trying to figure out if I have the right to be mad at him, them or not, I felt a warm hand being placed on my elbow and abruptly turning me around. That's when came in face to face with the same Greek god that is torturing me.

"what's wrong?" Ian repeated but this time his voice and eyes reflected a storm of emotions and they startled me and for once I was held a total captive to them

"Nothing" I stubbornly replied as he masked his emotions away

"Maya I know that something is wrong with you...There is no spark in your eyes...They are just dark." Ian insisted pleading to know what is happening in my head

"I didn't have enough sleep." I replied and it was a total truth I didn't sleep last night

"Did Asher do something wrong?" Ian became stiff and his grip on my hand tightened then brought me closer

"He did all the right things." I answered truly because Asher is a gentleman and secondly I wanted to know how will Ian react...Does he care even slightly?

"Then why didn't you get some sleep?" He sounded confused and somehow hurt?

"What do you think? What do couples do when they stay up all night together?" I challenged more and then felt Ian's grip loosening around my hand so I took a step away from him and ran to my office.

He let go of me. There was no reaction at all. He just stood and watched me leave! I guess he doesn't care at all about me. I guess he is Rose's always was and will always be.

They are forever.

"What did you tell Ian?" Nick asked as he rushed into my office as I continued to grief over my unwanted feelings for more than an hour

"Nothing but why?" I answered trying to pull a strong facade

"Well to say that he is angry is an understatement. And when I asked him about the reasons he grumbled your name." Nick replied and took a seat on the other side of my desk.

"I didn't do or say anything." I denied as I refused to believe that Ian got frustrated with my announcement/lie

"You two act all cozy and close then flip on each other. You are like a typical married couple." Nick joked and I was in no mood to hear the rest of his humor

"Well Nick if you don't mind I would like to go back to my files." I professionally said

"You will end up telling me what's wrong soon. But a piece of advice, let go of Asher nicely because you are clearly...." Nick tried to continue but saw Ian coming by

"Don't leave!? please.." I begged but Nick answered me only with this boyish grin and ran to his office

One,...should I leave my office?

two,...should I stay and ignore him or flip at him?

three,...should I act normally...after all, he is with Rose. Cheating but yes with Rose.

"Maya!" Ian spoke harshly as he entered my office and slammed my office door shut

"What?" I acted as innocently as possible because his angered expressions angered me

"Tell me that you wild night didn't happen!" he ordered as he walked to my side of the office turned my wheeled chair to him and bent down looking at me right in the eyes. I wanted to push my chair away from him. I wanted to break free from his gaze and his caging arms that rested on both arm rests of my chair.

"Why?" I asked again

"Just freaking tell me!" he spoke lowly but firmly

"You have no right to order me." I spoke firmly back at him and tried to push him away but he didn't move

"Maya..." Ian grumbled at me

"Why do you care! You are not supposed to." I questioned him as my own temper started to show

"The pull makes me..." Ian explained calmly after minutes of silence and continuous staring

"Well I don't see you yelling at Rose and she is the married one! God knows that your stupid emotional pull with her is much much much more powerful." I finally uttered letting my jealousy, my green eyed monster show.

"Didn't Rose explain things to you?" Ian sounded taken aback

"No need. After all we are friends, You were always in love with her and I am dating Asher. now if it is okay with you, I would appreciate it if you let go and let me get back to work!" I answered strictly and tried to push him away again but his hand rapidly circled around mine sending those stupid shivers and sparks all over my body

"I love Rose and will always do but the kind of love I have for her changed!" Ian uttered shocking me

" You discovered that after or before sinking low and kissing her even though she is married ?" I challenged him again

" never kissed her well not in a whole freaking year and a half. But you have no right to get this angry since you spent a wild night kissing, making out and doing gods knows what with Asher." he challenged back

"I have every right because Rose is my best friend and you made a cheater out of her! and poor Jacob his heart will be broken if he ever knows in what position I found you guys...But ask yourself why are yelling at me for spending a night with my date kissing, making out or even doing god knows what!" I fired at him and tried to push him away from me with my free hand yet he captured it and drew more close to him...Just one inch and our lips will be sealed together and our heart beats will mix and fuse

"Because...You are mine and should be mine and only mine." Ian explained possessively and something shinned in his eyes "You make me feel like a kid. You challenge me and your touch soothes me. Even Rose didn't have such intense powers on me but you...Your eyes, lips, curves, smile, words and mind...Dammit Maya, you came into my life so suddenly but changed it all and Now I can clearly see it I want you." Ian replied and I couldn't stop my heart from skipping beats

"I am not going to be one of your flings..." I grumbled at him but my only answer was a boyish silly grin...What's up with men and these silly boyish grins lately ?

"I don't want you to be a fling...I want you to be mine and only mine." Ian repeated then attached his lips to mine in a passionate sweet kiss and I couldn't but react instantly at him...Dear god how his kisses hypnotize me and make me feel like flying.

"I broke up with Asher last night...After I saw you with Rose...He and I both knew that I like another guy." I announced truthfully as I felt my cheek warming up and burning after our shared kiss

"What guy?" Ian asked playfully as he placed his finger under my chin and raised my head so I was looking at him in the eyes

"You..." I hushed and once again found my self lost in one of Ian's passionate kisses

So here you guys go :D

waiting for you comments to update

Thanks for reading, voting and commenting ^^

Little secret

Ian's Pov:

For the very first time, felt like I was doing the right thing. After kissing her and re-kissing and even giving her a hickey to show the world that she is mine, she threw me out of her office saying that we both need to work and that we had a conference in an hour. I hated the idea of not being with her...But I guess that I need to work...For hours, I waited for some alone time with her. For a long time, my eyes drifted to hers and my heart started beating in a new rhythm and I found in me a new kind of hunger...I was hungry for her eyes, lips, body, mind,soul and any type of connection with her. She gave me these small smiles whenever I looked her way and when I held her gaze for too long she blushed and looked away and I felt the happiest at those moments...What is she doing to me? Why am turning in this cheese ball?

"Lunch date." I sang/yelled as I entered Maya's office

"Hey" she replied without tearing her eyes from the papers she is reading

"May? lunch date?" I repeated and felt as bad as a kid being ignored or left out

"Sorry, Ian...I have this file to finish..You know that I haven't done much today..." she said and looked my way with those dark sparkly orbs of hers

"May.." I said and walked to her and her cheeks immediately turned red

"Nick needs this file..." she hushed as I turned her chair around as I did earlier and caged her between my two arms

"And I need you..." I whispered by her ear then started to leave a trail of kisses from her ear to her neck and heard her gasp

"Ian.." she moaned my name as I continued to kiss her

"You clearly want me too...So lunch?" I offered and she nodded agreeing and that made me grin

"You cannot do that again..." she started as we enjoyed our meals and I couldn't help but chuckle

"do what?" I teased knowing exactly what was her answer

"You know the kisses ...." Maya explained in coy way and it made me want to kiss her right there and then

"you don't want me to kiss you?" I teased her more and she started turning more red

"I didn't mean that" she hushed in a small voice and I barely heard her but that statement made me the happiest guy ever and as I leaned forward to steal one more kiss her phone beeped announcing that she got a text.

"It is Rose, she is asking how am I" May announced and then a troubled look appeared on her face

"Don't tell her about us...She might overreact" I replied and suddenly saw all of Maya's facial reactions changed

" Okay" Maya coldly replied

"It is for the best..." I promised

"okay..." Maya repeated

"Are you upset...did I say something wrong?" I honestly questioned no knowing what happened

"Nothing at all... because clearly I am nothing but a dirty little secret ...I won't tell Rose...I won't tell Nick and also none of my family members..." She kind of yelled

"Maya I didn't mean that..." I honestly replied

"Sure you didn't mean that...but I mean every word that I am going to say...Ian, I won't be your dirty little secret...I won't be your anything unless I know for sure that Rose is no more important than me...If you fear her reaction and care about her more than my reaction then I have to let you go...You made me the happiest in these few hours but if you want to keep me just as a hidden secret...then sorry but I have to much pride to be that..." Maya rapidly said as she stood from her chair and walked away

"Maya....Maya" I yelled after her as I threw some money on the restaurant table and ran after her...What have I done? Did I freaking lose her at the same moment I had her ?

"Maya..." I cried again as I saw her stopping a cab and getting in it

"Dammit!" I yelled and then ran to my car to go after her

The ride was the slowest ride ever. Cars popped out of nowhere and seemed to deliberately block my way. I felt stupid and lost! I didn't mean to hid her away from the rest of the world. I didn't think of her as a dirty little secret...but I didn't want to face Rose...I had no will to have her nagging around Maya about how self centered I am or how cruel am I or how am I a naturally born player that will eventually end up cheating on her!

I grumbled loudly as I entered the company and ran to her office people kept on watching me weirdly but I ignored all their stares and looks. I needed to reach her and I needed to do that fast.

"Maya." I exclaimed as I entered her office

"Ian" she coldly replied

"Maya you got me wrong..." I said but got no reaction

"How?" she asked coldly without looking my way

"I feared that Rose will convince you to let me go because I will hurt you or cheat on you or because I am not good enough for you..." I argued pleading

"So you don't think that I trust you?" She asked and I swear that I saw tears in her eyes

"I don't know...I mean I am not typically your type...I am anything but your type....You said it you won't dare date someone like me..." I replied remembering her once made announcement

"I said so...I know...But since the wedding you made me feel things that I never felt...You touch makes thousands of butterflies erupt in my stomach and I see fireworks when you kiss me...the pull that you talked about is mutual...I somehow feel safe when I am around you but if you are not willing to share that pull with the world then sorry Ian. I wasn't raised to be a dirty little secret..." she cried as she stood and walked to me

"I will never treat you as a secret I want the world to know that your mine...I hate how guys look at you and how nick hugs you or how Asher kissed you...I loathed that...But Rose..." I tried to explain

"When you are ready to face her and acknowledge us for the most important person in my life then I will be with you but for now Ian I don't believe that you are ready for a serious relationship." Maya hushed and then kissed my cheek and went out of her office leaving me behind like a lost puppy...What have done? how can I get into and out of relationship in the same day !

Waiting for your comments to write the next chapter !

Vote , comment and most of all enjoy :D

thanks for reading this

I Love You

I an's Pov

Tell Rose! all that kept on replaying in my mind were those words. I didn't focus at all for the rest of the day and knowing that Nick had called Maya to his office since lunch and she still didn't come back is driving me insane.

I like Maya that's final and I am falling for her. I need to fix our situation. As soon as I left my office I drove to Rose's house. I know that she will never believe my honest intentions and she might even convince Maya to stay away from me but I will deal with that later on.

For now I have a solo mission and that is telling Rose and showing Maya that I want to be with her.

As I rang the door, I started getting nervous. But what has to be done needs to be done. When the door swung open, I came face to face with a crying Rose. I might no love her in an intimate way anymore but my heart throbbed painfully at such a sight. Why is a beautiful sweet pregnant lady crying this hard.

"Ian" she sniffed saying and without a warning threw herself in my hands

"What's wrong?" I questioned her as I struggled to get her inside

"Jack! He hates me now." she yelled/ cried into my chest

"Why is that?" I questioned her knowing for sure that that man cannot hurt her at all

"I told him that you and I nearly kissed and he flipped." she explained and I couldn't blame the guy...

"I will talk to him, I promise." I tried to sooth Rose

"He will never trust you. He thinks that I am still in love with you! what am I going to do?" she cried as her head rested on my chest and I hugged her closer

"Show him that you love him." I replied and after that allowed her to silently cry on my chest

"You are the best Ian. thanks for helping through this..." Rose said as she straightened a bit and looked me directly in the eyes.

We were too close again. We were breathing the same air and her hopeless crying eyes made me sad a bit. I wanted to hug her and be there for her but just as a friend no more...But she clearly had a different idea. She slowly started to reach for my lips and my breaths hitched at this. Is she going to kiss me? Am I going to feel the same way? shouldn't she be kissing her husband? What will Maya do if she finds out? Smooth lips came into contact with the side of my lips and I closed my eyes enjoying even for the slightest moment the familiarity of such lips and intimacy.

"See" that all we heard and that made us jump away from each other and looking at the source of the sound I found Jack and Maya standing side by side with the same pained look on their faces.

"Jack..." Rose called in a pleading way

"Don't I will just take some of my stuff and head out..." he replied but couldn't careless about him or Rose now.

"I convinced him to come back saying that I saw what happened that day and that it was nothing..." Maya said in a small voice then a tear fell down her cheek and she rapidly wiped it with the back of her hand, turned around away from my apologetic eyes and ran away.

Maya's Pov

Now I know why he wanted to keep a hidden secret. Now I am sure of why he told me not tell Rose. I couldn't stop the tears from falling on my cheeks heavily. I couldn't stand there and watch them so I did what I do best I ran to my car.

"May...Maya...Maya" Ian yelled as he ran behind me, got a hold of my elbow and turned me around

"Let go." I yelled back and saw a mixture of emotions in his eyes

"You got it all wrong!" He declared and I couldn't but sarcastically laugh at him

"Yeah, It is always me. I always get everything wrongly." I said mockingly

"I didn't start that!" he spoke more calmly

"Sure you didn't...and do you know what I am glad because we didn't start a thing or else I would have been more broken." I informed him and tried to pull my elbow away from his hand but he wouldn't let go

" I came here to tell her about us..." Ian said as he tried to pull me closer to him

"But you found a better offer here, right? I mean she has always been your first love and one and only while I am just a means to get her..." I cried harder and felt my heart breaking at such truths

"May...I didn't do a thing." Ian promised again but I just couldn't believe him

"You will always be a player...and I guess that I am finally up to let my mum find a descent guy." I informed him and saw his orbs hardening and darkening in color

" No other guy will have you." Ian promised and threatened

"You do not own me or control me. Now let go of my hand or I will call Jack and he will certainly punch you." I threatened back

"I would love to see him try." Ian carelessly mocked my threat then pulled me closer to him and even when I tried to take a step away from him his hands were faster than me and in minutes they hugged my waist and brought me closer than needed to him. We were again face to face, breathing the same air.

"I didn't feel this way when she came to me. It is only you." Ian hushed and in seconds his lips found their way to mine and as much as I tried to push him far away from me his hands just tightened around my waist and held me in place. I tried my best not to kiss him back but that stupid pull, my anger and my confused emotions got the best of me and I just started to kiss him back in a harsh punishing way.

"I love you." Ian hushed as we separated from the kiss

"I don't trust you." I said and find a way out of his hands then continued to ran to my car.

hello you guys,

I need to ask you guys for a favor. I started this new book " Insane" ,after a sleepless night and tones of werewolf rejection romance books. It is called "Insane". I would love for you guys to check it out and comment your opinions there. This may be much to ask but I cannot get rid of this idea and I wanted to know your guys impressions about it so please check it out and tell me if i should continue it too.

thanks a million you guys are the best ^^

Comment and vote as usual

thanks a lot

Andy?

M aya's Pov:

After that crazy hour of non ending heartbreaking events, I cut off all what links me the outside reality and shut my self home. I didn't know what to do or how I should act. My mind kept on telling me to forget about Ian. But my heart even though broken kept on beating rapidly at the mention of that stupid man's name.

The image of them kissing replied in my mind again and again and every time it made my eyes water. Ian and Rose both kept on calling me and didn't answer them at all. When going to put my phone on silent mood, it rang again but the caller was neither of those former two. It was jack and my heart broke a little for him as I remembered how I convinced him that his wife adores him only, how he bought flowers and chocolates for her and was ready to ask for forgiveness. Yet the scene that met him ripped his heart apart and made him seethe in anger.

"Maymay..." Jack said sounding tipsy or even drunk as ever

"Jack where are you?" I questioned as I got tensed knowing that he is not used to drinking at all

"In a bar...I tried to forget her...I really did...But I couldn't....I love her...She is carrying my baby...But I guess I am not good enough for her." He ranted between hiccups and I felt pain imaging how this once strong man may look right now; broken, crying and lonely.

"I know Jack. I know...Jack how are you going back home?" I questioned him but there was only silence

"Jack?" I questioned again yet nothing

"Hello?" a different manly voice greeted after a second

"Hello, who is this?" I questioned rapidly in an alert tone

"This is the bartender of the bar "VIP", your friend here just passed out and I don't know exactly where to send him if I call a cab for him." the man informed me

"Give me the address. I will come and pick him up." I answered in a heartbeat because Jack has been one of my closest friends and he deserves to be saved after the harsh day that he had.

I dressed really quickly or let's say that I changed shirts and kept on my sweatpants, wear my shoes and left in a rush. I followed the instructions that the bartender gave me and in half an hour I was in front of this huge bar. The sounds that were erupting from it were different; songs, yells, loud laughter and the lights that illuminated it were vibrant and different. Entering to such bar wasn't the easiest thing. The line in front of it was long because this bar turned up to be the number one go to new bar. Stupid Jack even when sad he kind of does it with style.

When finally entering, different smells hit my nose and I found that most of them were revoking. I was never into alcohol. I couldn't bare loosing my conciseness and I don't even know how people can do that and make themselves so vulnerable. About vulnerability, I must find Jack then go back to my unfinished tub of ice cream. Searching around, I didn't see him anywhere. But suddenly I felt someone pulling my elbow and while I turned around I came face to face by none other than my heart breaker.

"What are you doing here?" Ian asked in a possessive kind of way and I glared at him angrily.

"None of your business." I yelled over the music and tried to pull my arm out of his tightening hand

"Let me drive you home." He ordered

"I ride only with people that I trust." I meanly said to him and saw pain and regret flashing in his orbs. I didn't want to hurt him but he already broke my heart and lost my trust.

"May, I swear I didn't do a thing." He promised again

"You could have pulled away. You could have pushed her away. But no, for the second time I catch you getting intimate and close with her and I cannot take that. I just couldn't live my life questioning if you will once again want her." I said brokenly and finally drew my hand away from his.

"May..." He uttered and even words failed him because I knew deep down he still loves her.

"Excuse me now but I have to go and correct the mess that you guys did." I informed him, turned around and went away in the bar's direction.

"What mess? What do you mean? Why are you here? May ..." Ian kept on following me through the sea of bodies and annoyingly asking thousands of questions but I decided to ignore him.

Catching a glimpse of Jack I ran to him. The view of him broke my heart. His head rested on the bar as he used his hands as a pillow. He seemed tired, exhausted even and some dry tears were still clear on his cheeks. Dear god this man is broken!

"Jack? Jack?" I tried to shake him awake but nothing

"Does Rose know about his state?" Ian asked as he watched me trying to help jack...his only concern is about Rose ! I nearly yelled at him but why embrace myself publicly for a man who doesn't care about my broken heart.

"Excuse me? Can I get a cup of water?" I asked the bartender

"Sure" he replied and in a second a cup was there on the counter waiting for me to give it to Jack

"Jack come on please drink this. So we can go." I pleaded him and he for once started to react.

"May?" Ian urgently called again but I ignored him

"Sweatpants for the most go to bar?" The bartender teased and that's when I directed my attention to him and took a good look at him. He was my age or probably a year older. He looked a bit like a surfer boy with blond curls and bright brown eyes.

"well they are the comfiest." I replied and sensed Ian taking a step closer to me

"Sure hell are, so you are the girl I talked to on the phone?" He asked and I nodded

"May let's go" Ian for a reason angrily hushed at me

"May that's a pretty name. I am Andrew by the way." the bartender Aka Andrew said offering a bright smile and an extended hard

"It is Maya and nice to meet you." I smiled at him and saw that Jack is kind of awake now

"Maya do you want some help with him? My shift just ended and I can take him to your car." Andrew offered

"No!" Ian roared at both us

"actually yes, I need some help." I corrected ignoring how close to me Ian got and how he acted so possessively.

"May." Ian now uttered in a hurt questioning tone so I turned to him and his eyes were full of different troubled emotions.

"Go home Ian." I sweetly ordered him as Andrew helped Jack up and waited for me to walk them to my car.

"So is that your boyfriend?" Andrew asked as we walk to my car

"He is ...It is complicated." I replied in a sad tone

"Who is this?" Andrew again questioned but this time pointed at Jack

"My best friend's husband." I answered introducing the latter

"Why did he call you? are you both like cheating !" Andrew continued his twenty questions game

"No, he is my other best friend and his wife and him fought." I informed him again

"So you have no boyfriend?" He asked as I opened the backseat's door for him so he can help Jack in

"Kind of..." I answered after a long silence

"Well..." Andrew continued after getting Jack in and slamming the car door shut "If it is okay with you I would love to get your number and see if we can go out someday soon."

"I...I..." I didn't know how to answer

"Her number is (number)" Jack ranted from the car window while showing Andrew his phone screen of my number

"Thank you buddy but I want her to give it to me." Andrew joked and put emphasis on "her" as I awkwardly gasped at Jake's friendly drunken nature.

" So?" Andrew asked and I couldn't help but think that this might be my chance at moving forward and starting something real.

"it is (.....)" I said giving my number and saw a friendly smile on Andrew's face

"Thanks Maymay." Andrew teased as he used the name he saw on Jack's phone

"Yeah...Yeah now goodnight Andy." I tried to tease him back and his smile just grew wider

"Goodnight." he replied back waved and started to take steps to a car near by

"Goodnight Andy." Jack yelled in seconds and that made Andrew and I chuckle in laughter

Here you guys go. I will be waiting for your comments to update :D

Can't wait to hear your opinions :D

thanks for reading commenting & voting ^^

Feelings

I an's Pov:

She left with that freaking bartender and I was left alone. Go home, she said but didn't she know that I couldn't. I just can't bare the idea of her with two other guys; one drunk and one well seems like a player. I hated the fact that I might have lost her forever. She seemed so determent to move on and to never allow me in through her walls again.

I tired to force myself back to my old seat in the bar but all that kept playing in my memory is how that bartender's eyes traveled along Maya's body studying it. How a flirting smirk appeared on his face when she accepted his help. My chair suddenly felt so tight and small. The air in the bar became thick and sickening. Even my stomach hurt. I didn't know what was happening but I felt like everything around me felt wrong.

The beerless glass in front of me looked as lonely and empty as my soul. Void was a common point between them. I ordered more drinks hoping to drown myself in anything but alcohol. One drink became two and then three. Yet nothing seemed to work. I am still hurting and my only comfort is Maya.

Maybe if I go to her now, beg for her and show her that I love her and only her, she may forgive me?

Even if my chances were close to nothing I decided to try. I tried to stand but dizziness hit me as soon as I supported all my weight and stood tall. Maybe I drank too much? Maybe I shouldn't drive? but what if tomorrow is too late? What if she drives back with Andrew? What if she and Jack...

No Maya would never do that! I screamed at my own racing mind and tried to slowly walk between the grinding bodies and the wild groups that kept on jumping with the music, swaying with its rhymes and singing its lyrics. It took all my energy to walk back to my car. Images of my surroundings were blurred. Colors were not that clear. Even the sounds were muffled now.

As I got into my car I rested my head a it on the steering wheel but those stupid images of Maya and Andrew making out kept on haunting me. What if she tires to forget me and use Andrew as a way? Will I be the reason behind corrupting her innocent soul?

Even though my body hurt and my limbs seemed to be heavier than normal, I started my car. Different voices played in my head, one saying that I should drive to Maya's fast, another saying I am too drunk to drive, and another cursing Andrew...The lights of others cars started to irritate my already blurred vision. My eyes started hurting me more and my head throbbed painfully. Yet I ignored it all. I ignored all pain and tried to reach Maya.

I was driving yet suddenly my blurred vision darkened. The cars around me didn't flash their lights in my face. I no more heard their annoying beeps. I heard nothing at all and saw nothing. I only felt some sharp pain. I wanted to ignore it too. I still wanted to find Maya but my body gave up on me and total darkness and silence enveloped me.

Maya's Pov :

After guiding Jack to the guest room, I returned to my now melted ice cream box. I threw the thing away. Then, I looked around me and my solitude finally hit me hard. I will always be alone. The only man that I wanted is in love with my best friend...Will I ever be good enough for anyone? Maybe Andrew will love me? But will I love him back? Will I ever feel the same way about him as I feel for Ian?

Ian, that selfish man, why did I fell for him? Why did my heart choose him out of all the guys in this planet? Why did my eyes twinkle in happiness whenever he is around? Why did my heart dance rapidly and wildly when he told me that he loves me? Why did I want to tell him that I love him too right away?

"I love you too." I mumbled and a fierce wild cry left my mouth. I felt my legs giving up on me and wobbly I sat on the floor hugging my knees to my chest and resting my forehead on them.

Will I die alone? Will Ian rush to Rose's side if Jack divorces her? Should I ignore Asher's texts or respond to him? why am I living in such a mess...

I don't know for how much time, I sat on the cold floor of my kitchen but I only woke up when I felt someone poking my arm. I grumbled and tried as hard as I can to lift my head...It seemed to weight tones...It hurts a lot...I guess because I spent the night crying my heart out. As soon as my eyes opened I met the face of a very concerned and troubled Jack.

"MayMay..." he mumbled and I saw tears forming in his own eyes

"Jack..." I mumbled back then a moment of silence took over us. That silence was anything but meaningless it seemed pregnant with meanings and messages and it made my eyes water again.

"He has been calling you endlessly for an hour." Jack announced surprising me

"He?" I asked not knowing who he is talking about

"Ian." Jack spat the name with a vivid anger and I couldn't blame him.

"oh..." was my only answer

"You fell for him. Didn't you?" Jack asked and I knew that he wasn't waiting for an answer so I just rested my head on his shoulder and allowed my tears to fall...We stayed like that for ten or fifteen minutes. Not a sound was made other than my sobs. Jack's comforting hand hugged me close and tried to sooth me but we both knew that nothing will work. We were both broken behind repair. My head lifted from his shoulder when I heard my house phone beeping. Yet I decided it to ignore it. I am in no will to talk.

"Maybe you should answer that..." Jack said but I just shook my head and then rest it back on his shoulder.

"They will just leave a message." I announced and that's when I heard the beep.

"Hello, This is Mercy Hospital, I am sorry to inform you that Mr. Mathews had an accident. We tried to reach the last connected Numbers on his phone and this seems to be one of the first two." The message ended and I froze. I was no more able to cry I was just totally numb...

Waiting for your comments to update

Enjoy, vote and comment :D

Actually Already In Love

M aya's Pov:

Mercy Hospital.

Accident.

Ian.

All those words played and echoed in my mind endlessly. I froze and couldn't move. I stayed there on my cold kitchen floor and became as numb as ever. What if lose him? What if he is hurt because I left him in bar drunk and ordered him to drive home? What have I done? My tears again found a way to appear and they were falling now endlessly. I cried or sobbed. I was totally lost.

"Maymay...May...MAY....Maya?" Jack questioned with clear concern

"I did this. If I just talked to him. If I just heard him..." I cried hysterically

"You did nothing. He pushed you away and hurt you." Jack answered as he hugged me and I sobbed into his shirt.

"He is hurt." I uttered

"I will drive you there. Go wash your face and we will go and make sure that he is okay." Jack promised and my eyes rapidly connected with his searching for any hint of untruthfulness.

"But won't that be awkward for you? Don't you like hate him?" I shakily asked

"Both him and Rose are at fault and I cannot say that I hate her...Let's just go." Jack tried to respond but his voice got muffled again by what I guess the memory of his wife kissing another man.

"Thank you." I replied hugging him

"You know that I will do anything for you. You are my best friend too, you know?" Jack announced and I couldn't but hug him closer.

"You are the best." I said then rapidly washed my face, changed my clothes and ran with jack to the car.

The ride seemed slow. All streets were loaded with cars. Jack tried his best to avoid traffic but even though he tried we seemed to be lost in a sea of cars. He seemed genuinely concerned and I loved that about him. But now was no time to focus on Jack. The man I love is laying on one of the hospital beds suffering from god knows what injuries. Those images yet again made me shiver. Tears in second filled my eyes and as soon as they fell I started to wipe them away. I want to hide them. I wanted to look strong but nothing worked my heart felt broken and out of repair. It stopped beating earlier but now it feels burdened and heavy. It simply hurts.

"MayMay...please don't cry." Jack begged as the car stopped in a red light.

"I cannot help it..." I replied brokenly and even my voice echoed with pain and hurt.

"He will be okay." Jack promised again

"I hope so." I said nodding

"Should I call her?" Jack asked after a silent minute

"Rose?" I uttered the name and suddenly all hate had vanished. I don't hate her or Ian. All hard feelings had vanished and were replaced by pure concern and love...

"Yeah. I mean after all they were...are in love." Jack explained and I wanted to tell him that Ian is in love with me now but for what use...So I just nodded and silently sat in the car until the hospital came into view and that's when my already in pain heart started to throb more painfully and I I couldn't but hold my chest as of fear of it exploding with ache.

"Ian Mathews." I rushed saying to the receptionist

"Room A120." She replied then thanked her and started running to the room.

I ran as fast as my legs allowed me but once I came face to face with the door of that room my legs froze. What if he is in too much pain. What if he is unconscious. What if he is in dangerous situation. Maybe this happened because of my stubbornness. Maybe if I just answered one of his phone calls he would be okay now.

"What have I done?" I murmured to myself

"This is not your fault MayMay." Jack replied in the lowest voice and that startled me

"I am scared...I love..." I said turning but then my eyes landed on a second figure behind Jack.

"MayMay..." Rose whispered and I didn't know how am I supposed to answer her

"I am sorry." The words escaped my lips then in a second I turned away from her and opened the door.

The figure that greeted me was that of Ian. He seemed , for once, weak and helpless and such scene didn't settle right in my mind. I saw some cuts and a cast around his arm and that made my eyes for the billionth time today burst in tears. I slowly walked to him but I was too afraid to wake him up. He seemed to be in too much pain so I decided to let him rest. After I don't know for how much time of pure silence colonized the scene. Yet once my fingers seemed to find one of Ian's curls on his forehead and as they came into contact with it trying to push it away from his eyes, those orbs of his shot open and he continued to gaze at me.

I didn't know how to react but all figures in the room seemed to be gone. All machine sounds seemed to get weaker and weaker. The only sound that prevailed was my own intense heartbeat. And call me insane but I had to do my next move. All my body was asking for it, for reassurance that Ian was okay. For the very first time I started to lean in first. I saw his eyes doubling in size but there was no time to read much into this. Suddenly my lips came into contact with his smooth lips. He froze at first but then started to submit to the kiss. The same intense fireworks and shivers rose and exploded in my body but out of fear of hurting him I drew away quickly.

"Sorry..." I said and looked at Ian to find at me in this unusual kind of way

"Are you okay?" Jack asked stopping the gazing contest that seemed to start between me and Ian

"I have been better..." Ian replied sarcastically and took us all by surprise ...Shouldn't he be nice to Jack. After all the he just shattered Jack's heart and stole his wife.

The conversations didn't last long and I took no part in them. Ian seemed to be happy when talking to Rose and Jack stood furiously throwing remarks between now and then. Then the latter man as if he had enough, he announced that he is going back home. Rose looked in great pain when Jack ignored her and walked past her. Maybe they need to talk before one of them can be physically hurt just like Ian.

"Jack could you please drive Rose back? " I questioned earning a death glare from Jack and a small thankful smile from Rose.

"Okay..." Jack mumbled like a kid and stormed away.

"Thank you...I owe you one and here these are my car keys. It is parked in front of the hospital so when you need to come home use it." Rose said and handed me the keys and I just nodded at her.

"Why did you kiss me?" Ian's voice echoed in the now empty room

"It all happened in a rush...I was afraid of losing you..." I announced opening my heart again to him and letting all my walls disappear.

"Maya... I know that I kissed you when you ran out of my car but that didn't mean that we are together...I am actually already in love with another girl." Ian mumbled those few words as nicely as possible and I didn't know how to react...

"Ian?" I uttered after a moment of shock and he just continued to look at me with those big eyes of his . His stare seemed lost and he looked so innocent and fragile right now. I didn't know what to do...did he really lose his memory ?

Comment & vote to get the next chapter

thanks a lot , have a great day

On a Date ...

I an's Pov:

It is been two weeks since the accident. Everyone is treating me nicer than usual and I couldn't argue with that. I mean who hates attention and care? Yet the only strange thing that has been happening is the amount of visits that Maya payed me. She seemed to care more than all and I found that disturbing. Shouldn't she be like in raged with me for forcing a kiss on her? Shouldn't she slap and run far away from because I used her to get to Rose?

I still remember how waking up to Maya's lips made me feel. I felt this intense tingly feeling erupting all over my body. I felt relaxed and even if my body pained me as hell I didn't care but then I remembered my solo mission: I want to get Rose back and starting something new with Maya will only ruin that.

The hurt that I saw in Maya's face when I questioned her kiss and how broken she seemed when I told her that I am already in love with rose became a hunting memory. The way her orbs turned obscure made me shiver. I knew that something was wrong with her and I truly hope that I didn't hurt her that much...Maybe I broke her heart by giving her false hope. I seemed to get frustrated whenever this legacy of thoughts seemed to erupt and for a reason or another I found myself stalking all of Maya's social networks or even trying to call her...Should I apologize?

Maya made it a habit to visit me each two days. For now I was brought back to my parents' house. My mum at first was surprised to see Maya at the doorstep. But in less than half an hour both women became best friends. I even saw my mum crying with Maya and hugging her. She was asking her not to give up on something but when I asked they acted as if nothing happened.

Maya was supposed to visit me today. I was still imprisoned by mum. She promised to keep me a hostage till I become well. I tried to prove to her that I am good now but seeing my still apparent bruises she forbade me from stepping a foot outside my house. My company was currently taken care of by Nick , the same guy who tried to sleep with Maya...She promised me that they are friends now...Best friends she said but I felt annoyed deep down when she started to numerate the good characteristics if his. That day I kind of acted tired just to get her to shut up about how great Nick is and how he fits greatly in her group and how creative he is. If didn't know better I would have said that I don't like to hear Maya talking about other guys but why would that be true? After all I am in love with Rose and Rose alone.

The clock announced that it one pm and usually right now I will hearing the sound of the doorbell. Maya visited me a day ago and now she should be here but all I continued to hear is pure silence. I waited and found myself shocked at how much I got used to Maya's visits. All she did around here when she came was to hear me nag about my mum, then bring me my favorite type of ice cream and sometimes I allowed her to share it with me. Maya is a nice girl and the guy who will steal her heart will be one lucky guy.

Ten more minutes has passed and nothing. A feeling of uneasiness started to take over me and thoughts , dark ones, of Maya getting hurt on the road started to play in my mind. I couldn't help but worry and even my mum started to question about Maya's whereabouts.

"Maybe you should call her." my mum proposed

"What if she grew bored of me? I mean she has every right to forget about me...It is not like I matter to her." I replied in a sad tone and it hurt me to know that the only friend that I had here has already gave up on me.

"You matter to her way more than you know..." My mother hushed and I was about to ask her what did she mean by that but my thoughts were interrupted by the sound of a ringing bell. Relief and happiness seemed to find away to my heart as I ignored my mum's yells for me to slow down and continued to run to the door.

I wasn't ready to see what was in front of my closed door and as soon as I opened it all air got knocked out of my lungs. There she stood dressed in this form hugging golden dress. It left all her neck and shoulders uncovered and her creamy skin was offered for any viewer to see. Her long legs were also uncovered the dress reached an inch above her knees. The scene in front of me seemed to have some sort of power on me and I felt things happening to my body that usually didn't happen this fast.

"Where were you?" that's all I manged to say and I knew that my hoarse voice unveiled all the passion and lust that I was feeling.

"Hello to you too." Maya answered as she shifted her weight from leg to leg and clearly seemed to be anxious and I knew exactly why...Because I was lusting after her while I shouldn't be. I knew that my intense gaze was nearly setting her dress on fire but I didn't care for now I really liked what I was seeing.

"Where were you?" I repeated in the same way and I did for some reason want to know where she was.

"On a date." she answered in an anxious tone and that's when I felt this hurtful pang in my heart and for a reason I felt broken and cheated on... What the hell is going on with me?

US & Ice cream...

Maya's Pov:

The cutest thing is happening right now! For some unknown reason Ian is acting like a kid. I as usual came to visit him but this time I was late. My mum obliged me to go on a date saying that Ian won't remember and that I cannot live on the vain hope of him remembering me...So after days of nagging I gave up and went to this date with Jason, her friend's son. The date was good. Even though I was clearly uninterested and acting like a drama queen, in the hope of driving Jason away...That man was nothing but a gentleman. He allowed me to pay for my share, tried to talk me into considering him as a friend and enjoying our time. And I did.

"Aren't you going to eat your ice cream?" I asked Ian who stayed silent since I announced my date.

"I don't want it." he grumbled at me and folded his hands at his chest. I thought that for a reason, he will remember me, yell at me for going on a date, get jealous and kiss me senseless but here he is acting like a kid because his "friend" aka me was belated by her date and didn't phone him to assure him that she is okay.

"Come on Ian, I know that you want this." I teased him as I sat beside him and waved the ice cream cone near his face.

"Nope." he grumbled again and continued to watch the TV.

"You two are cute." Ian's mum announced as she joined us.

"There is no we" Ian said as he ushered between me and him " I am not talking to her anymore." he continued to act like a baby

"Ignore him hun, he is just being a baby because you are the only one who is paying him enough attention...So how was your date?" His mum asked and I saw sadness flashing in her eyes...She knows I told her everything about Ian and I.

"I don't want to hear about it." Ian yelled and shifted a bit closer to me

"Then go to your room!" his mum ordered but he didn't move he just froze there and listened

"The date was good...My mum said that I cannot lose my time waiting...I tired to convince her but she started saying that she wants to make sure that there will be someone by my side before her death and that she wants to have grand kids and all..She even cried and that's why I said yes...Jason , my date, turned to be a total gentleman...He allowed us to act like friends the entire time the only thing he did was to hold my hand." I answered and felt Ian's hand brushing mine but as I looked his way he looked away and shifted away from me.

"He sounds like a good man..." Mrs.Mathews replied and I nodded

"I have to leave...I will buy some groceries and be back by half an hour." Mrs.Mathews continued to talk and Ian and I just nodded at her.

"That's my ice cream." Ian finally spoke breaking the weird silence that enveloped us

"Well you should have said so like a minute ago. It is mine now." I shrugged at him and continued to enjoy the heavenly frozen goodness in my hand

"You are mean." Ian huffed at me and folded his hands in a dramatic way

"Well you are being a kid." I replied to him and heard him huffing again

"Well you could have called." Ian answered back in clear anger

"Well I wasn't that late...and you shouldn't care" I fired back at him and that's when his body shifted and in a second his hand captured mine turning me side ways to face him and let me tell you that his eyes were dark and they made me shiver.

"I do care." Ian rumbled in the lowest tone and for a reason his hold tightened on my hand

"I care a lot." Ian repeated and that's when my cone of ice cream fell out of my hand

"can you let go?" I kind of begged because being this close to him is bringing back old memories, flashbacks of the office kiss, of how it felt ...I am going to break and cry if he doesn't let go

"You have some ice cream here..." Ian replied ignoring my request and his other hand came in contact with my cheek as his thumb traced the corner of my lips making me shiver and giving me thousands of fireworks.

"Ian...I should go." I barely spoke and what happened next froze me. The same warm lips came into contact with mine and the same familiar strong hands enveloped me bringing me to Ian's lap. I didn't know what to do but I in a minute started to react to his demanding lips. I lost myself in the kiss and my eyes like Ian closed. His hands tightened around me and then started to massage my back and I couldn't but moan his name...Then as if remembering his medical condition my tears started to heavily fall. I decided to back off. I should respect his state. I should let go because he said it clearly he is already in love. As soon as my hands tried to push away his chest, he grumbled and pulled me closer. Yet when my tears became noticed to him, he stopped.

"I am so sorry." I announced and tried to push away from his lap but he wouldn't let go

"May..." he replied in a weird tone

"I should clean up that ice cream and go home." I said in a low voice but he wouldn't let go

"Stay the night. I miss you." Ian said in a sincere tone surprising me...Does he remember us ?

deeply, insanely...

Ian's Pov

"please , stay ...

I miss you....

even for this one night..."

Those words escaped my mouth as I kept on watching Maya's features closely. Her eyes hardened a bit with doubt then became warmer with sadness and as I held her tighter her brown orbs shinned like glitter. Her lips turned from a frown to thin line to a hopeful smile. Little by little memories of me kissing her flashed in front of me and I couldn't but feel warm inside. This girl is really the fire in me.

"Ian, do you...?" her voice trembled and I knew what she wanted to ask

"Do I remember?" I completed for her and she nodded like a kid then captured her lower lip between her teeth and held her breath in fear of my answer

"I am sorry for all the heartache...I didn't kiss her." I confessed remembering the heartbreaking emotions that were reflected in Maya's eyes as she
witnessed that moment between me and Rose

"That doesn't matter now." Maya replied in a small voice and rested her
head on my chest and to that my heart started doing its own crazy dances

"It matters, everything does when it comes to you and that's why I need
to apologize..." I replied assertively because one of the few moments I can
recall are me saying I love you to Maya, me kissing her and her being heart
broken

"I am sorry too for the accident, if I just picked my phone ..." her voice was
getting smaller but her tone was heavy with guilt

"I was drunk no one could have saved me..." I assured her and hugged
her closer if that's even possible and we both fell into this comfortable
silence...No word was spoken, not a voice was uttered. We just hugged
and reconnected silently...How did simple girl managed to capture the
Casanova in me? How is she able to tame my player/ heartless part in me?
How did she pull me to her and erased every memory I have of Rose?

"Do you remember everything?" Maya asked cutting the growing silence

"Somethings are still foggy..." I honestly replied

"Foggy so you don't remember everything about....us?" she questioned in
a coy way and her cheeks blushed deeply...

"I remember the young us, our school, our not so friendly relation, your
bullies, me standing up to you, then years of separation and Rose's weddi
ng...Stolen forced kisses, me saying I love you and the heartbreak Rose and
I caused you..." I summed what I can recall and as I finished May withdrew
from my hands and looked at me questioningly

"You stood up for me?" she re-said with surprise and astonishment

"Yes, against Marcus...Rose came to me one day and said that he is bullying you because of your weight. I couldn't accept that and just faced him.." I explained to her remembering our school days and how rose told me that Marcus was calling Maya a "Fatty two shoes". Even back then I didn't like such behavior. I may be a player but I am not a bully. I do not make fun of people and even the girls that I used to sleep with fully know that I am not and will never be serious...but here I am now a changed person. The same guy but I fell truly deeply in love with a cute simple goody two shoes...

"Thank you" May uttered and in a rapid movement her lips captured mine in a fast peck

"You are welcome...So did you like your date?" I asked afraid of what to come

"It was nice..." Maya said but I guess my tightening grip alerted her

"Nice." I grumbled and started to push her away from my lap

"He was a true gentleman, took me to a small restaurant instead of those big fancy ones and held my hand ... " Maya continued teasingly as she sat in my old place on the couch as I stood up

"Such a gentleman..." I grumbled and turned to look at her

"He is great." She nodded with a playful glint in her eyes but playful or not I was jealous for sure..She has no right to go out with any other being ...

"Ha was ? " I questioned her as jealousy started to colonise my being and if she answers wrongly I will not be held accountable for my actions.

"Yup." She replied and nodded

That's when I trapped her between my hands as each rested beside her head on the couch and I started to dangerously leaning to her. Her eyes grew with surprise but the playful gleam in them never disappeared...Her smile grew and images flashed from our kiss in the office...When I was so blinded by jealousy...When I was madly angered by one of her dates...Am I going to live like this forever, always knowing that I love her but fearing that others may take her away? Just like Rose...I liked Rose but never officially committed to her...We just had an on and off kind of thing but she wanted more...

"Be mine, Be my girlfriend." Words yet again flew out of my lips but instead of freaking out I felt calm and happy "Be mine." I repeated and saw Maya blushing crazily and looking down in an attempt to avoid my intense gaze.

"I love you May and I don't want you to be anyone else's." I explained to her, held her chin delicately and positioned her head so she can look at me...I saw held tears in her eyes and I feared what may come...

"Even in front of Rose?" her trembling voice echoed in the room, reminding me of yet another scene...How stupid was I

"In front of the whole world...Be mine officially." I whispered at her and got this smallest nod. That was all it took for me to connect our lips together in a heated kiss... I love this girl...I love her with all my heart, deeply insanely wholly

"I love you too." She replied between taking breaths

Here you guys go :D

Enjoy

Don't forget to vote and comment <3

Perfect fit

- -

Maya's Pov:

"So are we going to stay here like this all day?" I asked as me and Ian continued to lay on the couch

"Well girls love to stay with their boyfriends like so for hours, at least from what I have seen in movies..." Ian replied explaining as he looked down at me and I couldn't help but tease him

"You are into chickflick, I would have never guessed." I uttered teasingly

"I am not, I just went on plenty of first dates." Ian answered rapidly and I tensed

"Oh..!" I said then stayed silent and tried to wiggle my way out of his grip

"I didn't mean to upset you...!" Ian said in a rush

"I know...It is just we are way too different." I honestly said as he allowed me to escape his hands and as I sat he did the same

"It never felt right to settle down. Yet when I held you for the first time, I got what it means to find your other half. You fit perfectly against me. It is like we were made for each other and no one can deny the chemistry and electricity that is between us..." Ian said as he scooted closer to me

"How many chick flicks did you watch again?" I teased him again even though my heart was beating loudly after hearing his words

"As much as I am going to kiss you now " Ian responded and in a swift move I was captured yet again by him

"Go get a room" Ian's mum interrupted us in a teasing tone and I couldn't help but blush and hide my face in Ian's chest

"Mother..." Ian grumbled clearly upset about his interrupted plans.

"Ian, sit we need to talk." she seriously replied and caught both in surprise

"Mum ? is everything okay?" Ian questioned as concern rose in him

"If you want I can leave?" I offered

"No Maya stay. You are a part of this too." She replied as seriously as ever

"Mum?" Ian repeated again in a questioning tone as his hand sneaked its way around my waist

"Ian, I just want to make sure that you know what you are doing with Maya. The girl have been hurt enough and even though you are my son and I should take your side, this time I can't. If you are going to break her heart I will personally stop talking to you. Before Maya, I did really admire Rose. I treated her like a daughter. Even though what you had with her never settled rightly...And you know that it hurt me to know that she cried over you for years. I was ashamed of what you did to her and had to apologize instead of you..Yet now if you break Maya's heart know for sure that no one will be by your side." She finished her speech and shot Ian a warning glare but he didn't seem afraid not at all

"I don't need anyone to be by me other than Maya. And Mother I must apologize to you but my promises won't be directed at you. I cannot promise you not to break Maya's heart. I cannot promise you to treat her rightly. I cannot promise you anything..." Ian said as he shook his head in denial and that made me fear for the future of our relationship

"Ian" he mother said with a warning tone

"Why can't you promise her Ian?" I said in hurt defeated tone

"Because" Ian said as he looked directly at me " I need to promise you and not the world. Better than that I need you to trust me and to know for sure that I won't hurt you." Ian replied and his eyes twinkled with new sparks

"I trust you" I promised

"fully?" he questioned as his smile grew

"madly and fully" I promised again

"And I love you madly and fully." He replied and started to lean down

"You must stop watching Chick flicks. You are as cheesy as they come." I teased as his lips nearly touched mine

"Mother" Ian yelled as a kid as he straightened his back and drew away from the kiss making me huff in disagreement

"Yes?" She replied seemingly having fun by the scene playing in front of her

"You need to fight for my rights too! she is bullying me because I watch Chick Flicks." Ian yelled and crossed his hand and his mum and I bursted in laughter

"May, play nice with him. He is too sentimental." She warned me playfully and walked to the kitchen

"This is so unjust! You are ganging against me." Ian huffed and I continued to laugh but after some silent seconds I looked at him and found his eyes sat on me and the intensity of his gaze made me blush.

"What?" I shyly mumbled

"You are beautiful when you laugh." He announced

"Yup my boyfriend is a cheese ball" I replied, stuck my tongue at him and ran to help his mum in the kitchen leaving him to grumble and making promises about payback.

Tomorrow Morning

"So what's going on? Why did you invite us to your mother's house?" Rose questioned Ian as she and Jacob (who are still working on their problems but at least civilly talking to each other and living under the same roof) came to have breakfast with Ian and I

"I want to tell you something but first let's eat." Ian promised

"Are okay Ian ? Did you get your memory back?" Rose question in the middle of our meal and owned her self a grumble from her husband

"Yeah Ian are you okay?" Jacob repeated with all the sarcasm that he can master

"You two need to relax." Ian announced then reached for my hand and I saw the eyes of Jacob and Rose doubling in size

"Ian? You remember?" Rose repeated again

"I do and I must tell you something. I don't want to ruin my chances again." Ian replied and smiled at me

"You are together aren't you?" Jacob said as he seemed to gain his voice

"Yes, we are and I need you to know because Rose is the most important person to Maya." Ian announced and Rose in a second yelled a "yeyyyyyy" and came to hug me.

"Congrats May and sorry for what I did before. I swear I have no interest whatsoever in Ian. It just my hormones and I felt lonely when Jacob left me alone and ..." Rose tried to hold back her tears and I just shushed her, hugged her back and told her that it is okay now

"I swear those girls care about each other more than they care about us..." Jacob noted jokingly

"Now they will need a girls day to catch up and I won't be able to continue the plans for May and I's first date..." Ian grumbled but a smile never left his face

"You became her type. The perfect fit." Jacob announced and Ian brightly smiled at him

"I am trying because she is my perfect fit " Ian agreed and winked at me making me blush

the end